THE JOCKEY & HER HORSE

ONCE UPON A HORSE

BOOK TWO

ONCE UPON A HORSE

THE JOCKEY & HER HORSE

BY SARAH MASLIN NIR & RAYMOND WHITE JR.

art by LAYLIE FRAZIER

cameron kids

CAMERON KIDS would like to thank Abriana Johnson, of Black Unicorn Creative and creator of *Black in the Saddle*, for reviewing this story.

Library of Congress Cataloging-in-Publication Data available.
ISBN: 978-1-951836-69-6

Printed in China

10 9 8 7 6 5 4 3 2 1

CAMERON KIDS is an imprint of CAMERON + COMPANY

CAMERON + COMPANY
Petaluma, California
www.cameronbooks.com

To my hero, Cheryl.
—S.M.N.

To my Father, my idol and role model.
To my Mother, my biggest cheerleader.
And to my sister, Cheryl, the legend.
—R.W.JR.

Chapter One

JETOLARA

CLANG!

Jetolara's head shot up. A few strands of scraggly grass clung to his lip. It was still dark out. But at the far edge of the field in which the horse stood, a warming, peachy light had begun to edge its way across the paddock. Dawn.

CLANG!

All around him, horse heads swiveled. The herd of a dozen horses straightened and stretched. They pulled their muzzles up from the dew-damp grass and pricked their ears toward the sound. The glow of the rising sun had not yet reached the corner of the pasture where he stood. Jetolara grazed a little ways off from the other horses, since he was as yet a stranger to them. It was still chilly where the thoroughbred stood. He watched enviously as the early rays caught their coats and turned rust red to bright cherry chestnut, dusky black to glinting ebony, and moody brown to the finest mahogany.

Far from the tight knot of the herd, he didn't dare move into their turf, even to catch the warming light. He remained in the last of shadows, where a withered old buckeye tree blocked the sun. It had pelted him with its pied nuts all night as he dozed beneath it. The night's chill had seeped under his chestnut fur. Jetolara shivered a little at the draft. Or maybe it was the newness of all of this—a new farm, a new herd, a new life for the young horse, in a place called Ohio, far from the Kentucky bluegrass where the thoroughbred was born—that gave him the chills.

CLANG!

His tail shot straight out. Maybe his shivers were really from that freaky noise!

But the other horses, clustered in a gully at the paddock's other edge, did not seem to be disturbed at all. Jetolara studied their reaction to the mysterious sound echoing from beyond the farmhouse washed in gray that stood on the hill. His stance relaxed a little. The others did not seem worried at all.

Actually—they were psyched!

All around him as the sun splashed out across the acres, the thoroughbreds in the field were coming to life with excitement. They shook out shaggy manes. They kicked their heels into the soft turf. They stomped hooves and snorted foggy plumes into the cool morning air. Jeto's big brown eyes went wide, till the whites were visible around the edges; what was getting everybody so riled up? He lofted his fine, tapered head into the air like a periscope, swiveling it around.

Horses have the biggest eyes of any land mammal, set wide on either side of their wedge-shaped heads. Jeto's eyes were no exception; they were the warm color of a cup of coffee, swirled with caramel, and didn't so much catch the sun as seem to give off their own spark. Peer as he might, Jetolara could not find the source of the herd's excitement. Nothing!

But Jeto could sense the tensed muscle in every thoroughbred around him; and his big ears, made so perceptive for safety in the wild, could even hear the slight uptick in the herd's pulse. Instinctively he stilled himself, too, and bunched every muscle in his body. Horses don't speak to each other as people do, but they communicate through their bodies. Those silent messages are as clear from horse to horse as a person saying "Pass the sugar, please" is to someone at the same table.

The herd around him was saying one thing: get ready to *run*.

CLANG!

They were off! And they were running *to* the noise! A big gray mare was first. From his vantage point under the buckeye, Jeto had noticed how that mare kept every horse in the field in line that night: she had doled out shooing nips to the babies who wandered off and scritches on the hard-to-reach shoulder blades, called withers, of her sister mares. Everyone else had dozed, sometimes standing with a foot cocked, sometimes dropping to their bellies with their chins lolling against the earth. She stood watch.

Each band of horses has such a queen. She is known as an alpha mare, and it is she who runs the show, with a stallion as her teammate, like the president and vice president of their community. The big gray alpha mare was a dedicated protector, and the herd was her life. It did not matter to her that the thoroughbreds lived far from the wild on a racehorse farm in a town called Rome, Ohio. There, even the Grand River seemed to slow down as it passed their pasture, just to linger a little while in the peace. The alpha mare's desire to keep her family safe was wrapped around her DNA more tightly than baling twine around a bushel of alfalfa.

But the alpha was easy now this morning, even in flight. She wasn't running *from* something, Jetolara swiftly realized. She was running *to* something. Soon, her almost white form was lost in the morning mist rising off the ryegrass below her hooves. She outpaced her herd, but they were not far behind. Thoroughbreds all, and in their very fiber built for speed, the animals streamed with her same happy abandon across the field. The sprint became a stampede. They flattened the purple bee balm buds and white trillium blooms that had dared to crop up over that early-spring night with the thunder of their hooves.

As the herd streamed away, Jetolara became nervous; a horse alone in a field with only a buckeye tree for company was not a good move; he could smell the fug of bobcats from the forests of Shawnee State Park near the paddock's edge. He wanted to run with the herd, even though they had not yet accepted him, but for another reason, too: if a horse does have reason to use their one weapon—a kick—it's best to be in front of whatever might want to snack on you. A hind hoof is only a good weapon if your threat is in your dust. Horses all know this, not because they are taught, but because it is a truth inside them, passed down through their blood.

Every hair of his chestnut coat, every strand of his rust-red mane, and every drop of hot blood inside of him screamed: RUN, JETOLARA!

Divots of spring grass exploded into the air as he blasted off.

Hot on their heels, as late a start as he got, the young horse soon closed the space between them with the powerful thrust of his haunches. In a flash, he had caught up! The whisks of their tails flicked his nose and flecked mud on the bright white stripe that ran down his forehead like a stroke of fresh paint. With a shove of his muscled shoulders, he bumped between them, ignoring the gnashing teeth and furious looks that said, in horse: *"Who do you think you are, stranger?"* He stretched out his long legs in a blistering gallop and, in a moment, was running at the big gray mare's side.

Then, Jetolara coiled like a spring, launched himself harder. He overtook her.

As the big barn at the foot of the pasture came into view, Jeto felt so powerful, so wild and free at the front of the herd, almost as if he were its alpha, that he would have soared over the paddock gate without noticing and kept running. That was how good it felt.

Then—CLANG!

That noise! So close and so loud that the young horse stopped so short his back hooves skidded beneath him, leaving furrows in the dirt. The other horses, more sensibly, had already slowed to a gentle stop behind him. As he stood stock-still, perplexed, the gray mare bumped his rump with her nose, nudging him onward. He craned his long neck back to peer at her, and what he saw deep in her eyes was respect. Jeto took a deep breath as he turned back toward the barn. Relief that he was on his way to joining the herd sighed through him.

Standing at the gate before him, with a metal pail in one hand and a feed scoop in the other, was a girl of about fourteen. Jeto realized that the tremendous sound that carried over the fields to the sleeping herd had been her knocking the two items together. "Whoo-ee, boy, I just watched you outpace Savannah Lily, and that gray mare once was the fastest horse we ever had," the girl said as she stepped forward, holding the pail out to his white-tipped muzzle. "Are you going to make my kid brother a famous jockey one day, boy?" Jeto sniffed the bucket skeptically, then excitedly: it was filled with oats!

His quick thoroughbred mind put it together: all that noise had meant BREAKFAST! And just as swiftly, he vowed from this day on that he would always be first whenever he heard that scrumptious CLANG! As he crunched on the breakfast in the pail, the herd hungrily jostling behind him, gingerly, gently, the girl slid her hand along the white stripe between his eyes. "Good boy, Jetolara," the girl said in a soft voice as she traced the whorl of white hairs on his forehead. "I'm Cheryl." The two-year-old thoroughbred had been at this farm just one day, but the touch was so kind that he suddenly felt, at last, at home. The feeling was almost better than oats, Jeto thought. Almost.

His nose deep in the oats, Jetolara revised his earlier thought: he would always come in first—*for Cheryl*.

Chapter Two

CHERYL

It was Cheryl's turn to feed the herd that morning. But every morning since forever she had been at the barn at dawn, even before she was big enough to carry the pail. Back when she was too small to toddle from their farmhouse at the top of the hill to the stables, her mother, Doris Jean Gorske, had toted her back and forth in her arms. Together they'd check that the racehorses had fresh hay and their water buckets were topped up, and then Doris Jean would head to work at the Ball jar factory in town. Later, when she was a toddler, Cheryl would go hand in hand with her father, Raymond, to check on the newborn foals or examine a horse with an injured foot. Cheryl couldn't imagine life that did not begin before sunup in the company of horses. It was not because that was all she had ever known, but because she loved the horses her family cared for, raised, and raced so, so much.

But her favorite mornings were when her father would lift her up and sit her atop his shoulders. That was when they'd head out to the field where the horses overnighted. Cutting through the green pasture was a path of soft dirt, a giant loop that ran at the perimeter, encircling many acres. That was her father's personal racetrack, beaten into the dirt over the years by the hooves of the racehorses he had trained, the racehorses his father trained before him, and those his father's father had trained, too.

With Cheryl atop the crow's nest of his shoulders, she had a bird's-eye view of the track. Her father would lean over the rail, stopwatch in hand, and together they'd watch as the men who worked for him exercised his racehorses. Dad would keep mental notes of each animal's development—who needed to build their stamina just a bit more, who needed to take it easy, and who was ready to race. From her high perch Cheryl also took mental notes of how the riders held themselves in the saddle, how they positioned their feet, how they used their hands and eyes. That was because in her mind, she was not perched on her daddy's shoulders; she was astride a great thoroughbred, too. In her mind, Cheryl was a jockey.

Not that she ever dared breathe a word of her fantasies to Raymond White Sr.—her daddy, the famous horse trainer—the man who had bred some of Ohio's best racehorses, animals that had sprinted in the most famous race of them all, the Kentucky Derby. Jockeys came from across the globe to train with him. The air at the backside of the tracks, the area where the jockeys mounted, was punctuated with foreign languages, like Spanish and French and German: "¡Ándale, ándale!" "Vite, vite!" "Schnell! Schnell!" "Go on! Go on!" the jockeys encouraged their horses in their mother tongues. Raymond White's legend was so large that a prospective client once sent an armored Rolls-Royce to fetch him from their farm, shocking the entire village of Rome, Ohio, population ninety-three. (Well, ninety-four if you counted Cheryl's annoying kid brother, Raymond Jr.—which she didn't.)

Everyone called Raymond Jr. by his nickname, "Drew," which had come from his middle name, Andrew. (Cheryl, of course, told him it was because the name sounded like "drool.") Raymond Jr. was part of why Cheryl kept secret her fantasy about becoming a jockey. It was a secret she held in her chest even now, at age fourteen. That was because Drew was a boy. In fact, except for Cheryl and her mother, Doris Jean, everyone who worked at Raymond White Racing Stables was male. Certainly, every one of her father's jockeys was. And so was every jockey Cheryl had ever seen at all the races the family had attended as they traveled with their horses across the country. It was the 1960s, and the rules of racing said only boys could grow up to be jockeys.

Cheryl had grown up riding ponies in the fields of the White family farm—fat Shetlands that were steady and kind and that she had trained herself. But she had never been allowed to train on a racing thoroughbred. Her father did not see the point: a girl could never ride in a real race. In fact, since thoroughbred racing began, only men had ever been allowed to become officially licensed jockeys. And that held true even now—in 1968—the year fourteen-year-old Cheryl met Jetolara. The year she realized she was desperate to race.

Jockeys have to be tiny. As a toddler on her father's shoulders, Cheryl had felt like she towered, but he was in fact quite short, the perfect size to ride fleet horses. In most races, official rules allowed no more than 124 pounds, including the saddle, atop a young racehorse. Cheryl remembered the exact number from the jockey's handbook just as she remembered every number she saw. She had an uncanny knack for sums and figures ever since she first learned to count. On long days at the track, when her father had his horses and his clients' horses running in races from dawn till dusk, she passed the time playing with the numbers she saw around her. Like the numbers on the pads under the horse's saddles, called towels: the number 5 on the green saddle towel of a lanky bay mare; the number 12 on the red saddle towel of the palomino balking at the starting gate. Using the numbers in front of her, Cheryl added and subtracted and divided and multiplied, just for fun.

Flicking sums through her head as she stood on the sidelines helped her dwell less on how jealous she was of her father's jockeys. How impressive they looked, dressed in their white silks with the Raymond White Racing Stables' signature red polka dots on their sleeves and his monogram emblazoned on their backs:

She wanted to be one of them.

The slim racing saddle and its rugs and weights couldn't be more than about six pounds, so she figured, $124 - 6 = 118$. The jockeys couldn't weigh more than 118 pounds. That was why most of them were short like her dad; it was way easier to stay that light if you were already small.

If Drew was annoying, it was through no fault of his own. It wasn't because he and his pals pinged her with spring apples when she walked to the orchard behind their farmhouse to pick the fruit for the horses. The boys would hide in the gnarled trees, climbing up them to pretend they were knights in high towers, waving branches as if they were swords. It was a favorite prank: when they saw her coming, they'd pluck the tiniest apples from amid the branches and drop them—plunk!—down on her, giggling like mad. Cheryl wasn't too bothered; sure, she'd holler at them for beaning her, but she'd collect the apples they dropped to feed to her horses, and in his goofy way, her brother made the chore a little simpler and a lot sillier.

What made Drew so annoying was this: Drew was over eight years younger than her, but even at age seven—in fact, ever since he was born—their father bragged to everyone about Raymond White Racing Stables' future star jockey: Raymond White Jr., *his boy*. It crushed Cheryl that by the simple fact of his gender, it was Drew, not her, who might one day ride a great horse like Jetolara into the winner's circle.

If she couldn't ride thoroughbreds, Cheryl would find another way to stay involved with the horses she loved so dearly. So, she threw herself into the world of horse training. As she grew up watching from atop her father's shoulders, Cheryl used her mathematical mind to learn how to tell future legends from horses who would never win a race. Now her brain sped with equations as she timed the sixteen-foot span of each galloping stride the animals took against her father's stopwatch. She then divided those strides into the 660 or so feet that make up a furlong—the unit of measurement used on every racetrack. She flabbergasted her father and his jockeys when she didn't need pen or paper to figure out which horse was their next winner. When she grew too tall to sit on his shoulders, her father bought her a stopwatch of her own, and they'd monitor and discuss the family's horses side by side at the rail.

That summer in 1968, Cheryl had reached her full height and had stopped growing. Her own numbers stood out to her: she was exactly five foot three inches tall and weighed 107 pounds.

Cheryl did the math. She was the perfect size for a jockey. But Cheryl was a girl.

Chapter Three

THE TRAPDOOR

When you live on a farm, there is no "I'm bored." There is no staying inside. You don't come in from sunup till it is pitch dark outside. The four hundred acres of the White family farm was a hive of activity. There was grass to cut and stalls to muck and horses to feed and fences to mend and tack to scrub . . . and when you were done with that, you started from the top all over again!

But in between, for Cheryl and particularly for her kid brother, Drew, there was mischief to make in the fresh air, and the fun was limited only by one's own imagination. In the middle of one pasture, little Drew trod out a baseball diamond for the neighborhood kids to scrimmage on, pulling on his mother's riding boots to stomp out the lanes between the bases in the grass. When the other kids were not around, Drew would run the bases with his dog, a Shiba Inu named Sheba who was the color of a nectarine. Meanwhile, in the barn, Cheryl hung a bucket with the bottom cut out from the rafters—when the horses finished breakfast and cleared out, it was the perfect all-weather basketball court, with the bucket as a hoop, for a pickup game with her friends.

Her best friend of all was Earlene Hill. They were exactly the same age, lived exactly across the street from each other, and sat side by side in homeroom at Grand Valley High School. Both of them could sing all the lyrics to Aretha Franklin's hit, "I Say a Little Prayer" by heart. They both loved watching It's Academic, a television quiz show on which bright students from across Ohio got to compete in a trivia contest. The two girls were similar in yet another way:

unlike most of her other friends in Rome, Earlene had the same dark skin as Cheryl, her father, and her brother. But where Cheryl's mother, Doris Jean, was white, and her father, Raymond, was Black, both of Earlene's parents, Mr. and Mrs. Hill, were Black.

Perhaps that was why one night, when she and Earlene were settled on their bellies in front of the television in the Hill house, propping themselves on their elbows on the carpet to watch *It's Academic*, Cheryl turned to her best friend. "Earlene, can you help me with something?" she asked.

For a moment, Cheryl's chin trembled a little. She swallowed. At school that afternoon, a boy had reached out during recess and touched her soft, kinky hair. His hand drew back as if he'd been stung. "What is wrong with your hair?!" he had exclaimed. Cheryl had put her hands to her scalp, feeling all around—what could he mean? She squeezed her eyes shut with embarrassment. Maybe when she'd fed Jetolara and the herd that morning she'd gotten a piece of hay tangled? Or worse, maybe one of the cardinals that roosted in the rafters had left a little surprise in her hair, and she hadn't noticed? How mortifying.

But what the boy said next was worse than a gallon of bird droppings: "It's all . . . coarse! It just grows like that? Ain't nothing you can do to fix that mess?"

Cheryl was shocked. When she curried and brushed her family's horses to a gleam each day, she noticed the patterns in their coats, the swirls and eddies of fur, the fine strands of some manes and thick fronds of others. There was the bushy tail dusting the heels of one gelding, the slim whisk of another tail flicking from behind a mare. All creatures were distinct, and all were beautiful to her; being different didn't make any of those horses *worse* than another. And yet this boy in her class thought her hair, her natural hair, was a mess?

Cheryl had looked around at her classmates hurling dodgeballs across the schoolyard or drawing hopscotch grids with chalk. Their hair fell straight or in waves, like her mother Doris Jean's, smooth to the touch, and except for Earlene, their skin was light like her mother's. Even though her brother, Drew, had darker skin like her, his hair was more like their mother's than Cheryl's. Cheryl's was thicker, and when she brushed it each morning it puffed out like a pretty halo, framing her face. When she put on her riding helmet and popped her poofy ponytail out the back, she had sometimes noted the difference. But it was not until that moment that she thought of Drew, of her mom, of her classmates, as having somehow— good hair?—and did that make hers . . . bad?

On the dodgeball court, few classmates had hair like hers, but in fact, few people in her life looked like her—or Earlene, or her father, or Drew. This was true not just at school, but also in the stables, at the racetracks, on the horses' backs, and in the bleachers cheering the thoroughbreds on. Her father was the only Black horse trainer she knew, she realized, and aside from Drew's promised future, she'd rarely read about Black jockeys in the *Daily Racing Form*, the horse-racing newspaper her daddy got delivered every morning to their silver mailbox out front.

That moment that boy grabbed her hair and sneered at her made Cheryl feel wildly out of place, not just at Grand Valley High School, but also in the racing world that had been her home since before she could walk. In every important way, the people in that world—from those cooling out the horses in the backstretch, to those rooting the animals on from the owners' boxes—were exactly like her; a community of humans bound by their shared love of horses. But almost no one looked like her. There at school, for the first time, she asked herself: why?

But there on the carpet at the Hill house in front of the television, she asked her best friend something different: "Earlene, how do I get good hair?"

The question sliced over the chatter of the television. Earlene shot up from the carpet. Cheryl was her best friend, the strongest girl she knew; she had watched Cheryl lift bales of hay by herself that would stagger grown men and do a layup on the bucket-basket in the barn. Cheryl was also the smartest girl she knew; she could do their calculus homework in her head and get more questions right than the contestants did when they watched *It's Academic*. Heck, that evening Cheryl had been over tutoring Earlene for the SATs! The idea that someone made her best friend feel that anything about her wasn't "good" enough was ridiculous to Earlene. In fact, it made her mad.

When Earlene spoke, without meaning to, it was with her voice raised. "You can only be you, because everyone else has been taken," she told her friend. Earlene's confidence was a gift from her mother, Mrs. Hill, who had endured similar taunts. Each bedtime, when she wrapped her daughter's springy hair in a silk cloth, she whispered to Earlene of her beauty and challenged her child to love herself as much as her mother loved her. Earlene shared hair like Cheryl's, but her mother had given her the confidence to know there was no such thing as "good" or "bad," just different. Earlene gestured to the screen, where a boy about their age was whizzing through questions on geography and buzzing in American current events trivia faster than any other contestant, to applause.

"You think that he got to be a star on *It's Academic* because he worried what rude kids at school thought about him? No! He was too busy working on himself to pay anyone any mind." Earlene took a breath. Then she softened her tone. Earlene patted the side of her own Afro, striking a fashion-model pose that made Cheryl giggle. "To work that hard on yourself, Cheryl, you have to love yourself."

Cheryl looked down at the thick shag pile of the carpet and picked at a strand. There in front of the television, the passion in Earlene's voice made her see herself through her friend's eyes. She thought about all the times she didn't love herself; like when she cursed being born a girl and wished she were a boy like Drew, so she could be a jockey one day. *You can only be you, because everyone else has been taken*. Envying Drew wouldn't get her closer to being a jockey. Allowing that boy to change how she felt about her hair? No way. *You have to love yourself*.

The newscaster voice of Don Cameron, the host of *It's Academic*, cut through the silence between them. "Question: which United States Olympian successfully sued the Maryland Racing Commission for denying her jockey's license application because of her gender, this year?" The boy they'd been rooting for buzzed in swiftly. "It's Kathy Kusner!" he said triumphantly, winning the round.

Cheryl's mouth fell open as she heard that trivia answer. It was 1968. She couldn't believe her ears. Could that be true? It had to be if it was on *It's Academic*! Women had just won the right to ride, thanks to whomever this Kathy Kusner woman was. The two friends stared at each other and began to giggle.

"WHOOP!" Cheryl shouted into the living room.

Whoever this woman was, Earlene wisely pointed out, she loved herself and knew her worth enough to fight so that others could know it, too. The friends promised each other to look up everything about Kathy Kusner and her fight with the Maryland Racing Commission in the library at Grand Valley ASAP.

When their excitement ebbed, and they could breathe normally again, Earlene reached across the space between the two friends. She took a piece of Cheryl's hair in her hand. She held it between her fingertips the way a person panning in a river might when she finds nuggets of solid gold, just to watch its beauty gleam. "Once you love yourself—the world is yours."

The next day, as surely as the sun rises and the cardinals tweetle it "Good morning," Cheryl's chores started over again. It was her turn to call the horses in for feeding time. They came as they always did when she clanged the feed scoop and pail together as their breakfast bell: a riot of colors and hooves and snorts and whinnies from where they slept at the far end of the pasture. Savannah Lily ran, keeping everyone in line. She was just behind Jetolara, who was working up a lather to stay a horse-length in front of the entire herd. He had been at the farm three months now and had earned the respect of the herd fully. He slept among them in safety and galloped with them in their joy.

Cheryl paused in her feed routine to give him his forehead scritches, as always, and he leaned into her palm, then stamped—a bit rudely, honestly—to tell her breakfast wouldn't serve itself, and he was *hungry*. She always marveled at how the horses knew exactly where to position themselves in the barn. After the frenzy of the run to the breakfast bell, they neatly arranged themselves in the aisle, filing in as tidily as students at Grand Valley were taught to line up to head to the cafeteria. Each horse ended up standing before his or her own bucket, which hung from hooks evenly spaced along the barn walls. Each morning the thoroughbreds claimed their same designated spot and guarded it zealously.

Clever Jeto had done one better—he had managed to claim the feed pail that hung directly below the trapdoor to the hayloft above. That was where Cheryl would do her next chore: throwing down flakes from the big bales of timothy and alfalfa stored up there to the hungry horses below. In that spot, Jeto had a front-row seat: when the hay came raining down, he would be the first to grab a mouthful.

With every pail full of oats and the horses crunching happily in the barn below, Cheryl climbed the sawdusty ladder up to the loft. It was peaceful, and sometimes she would take a break up there. She would count the hundreds of rays of slanting light that slipped through cracks in the timber framing, the dust sparking through them, and multiply them as if they were tally sticks. Today hay was piled to the roof—a new shipment had been stacked the night before—and she began to count the hay bales and multiply them, getting lost in numbers and the cheeps of the cardinals who nested among the bales.

Then she heard it. It wasn't the chirp of her state's beloved bird, the little song that flitted around the farm and was such a part of Raymond White Racing Stables that her father's jockeys wore silks of red—Cardinal red—as they rode. It was a bird's cry of pain.

Worried, Cheryl cast about among the bales, looking high in the eaves of the hayloft and low through the cracks in the floor for the distressed bird. Then she spotted it: halfway to the ceiling, in a tower of bales just beside the trapdoor, was a blur of red fluttering. A cardinal—its wing pinioned between two massive bales of alfalfa—must have been caught flying across the loft as the workmen flung the heavy loads of hay into stacks.

Quick as a filly out of the gate, Cheryl raced to the rescue. She hooked her fingers into the twine that wrapped each bale and climbed up the tower of hay to where the precious little bird was flit-flitting and cheep-cheeping helplessly. When she got to it, ever-so-gently, so as not to crush the creature, she pried up the bale on top and then pushed it slightly back, freeing the wing. In that instant, the wisp of a bird looked deep into Cheryl's eyes with its own black beads. Cheryl felt an unspoken thank-you just before the bird flew away, unharmed.

Then the tower of hay toppled.

Cheryl was falling, tumbling, bracing to hit the slatted hayloft floor and surely get the wind knocked out of her. But she did not. Because right below her was that trapdoor.

And right below that trapdoor was Jetolara.

She landed on his back with a thud, his withers slamming into her chest. The breath disappeared from her lungs, and she reached almost instinctively to wrap her arms around his neck. To the thoroughbred beneath her, whatever had just landed on his back did so just as a coyote would have, clamping onto his shoulders and, he thought wildly, trying to make a snack of him! And so Jetolara did what his cells and sinews and bones and breath had for generations told him would bring him to safety: he ran.

The chestnut galloped out of the barn with Cheryl clinging to his back, still unable to catch her breath. He flew down the pasture, his hooves trampling Drew's baseball diamond. He blasted past the buckeye tree and, alongside the Grand River, outpaced the current with every bounding leap. When he hit the track on which Cheryl's great-great-grandfather had ridden horses, and every man in the White family since him had, too, he did what thoroughbreds do best: Jetolara raced. Cheryl was gasping now, braiding her fingers into his rust-red mane, hugging her strong legs around him—he was going too fast to risk falling off—and becoming aware of shouts coming from the family farmhouse. Her father screaming, "Stop! Oh, dear Lord, Doris Jean! It's Cheryl! And Jeto! JETOLARA, STOP!"

Without a bridle or a saddle, Cheryl could no more stop the careening thoroughbred than she could stop a cardinal from singing. But as her breath steadied, and the warm back of the animal plunged and coiled beneath her, she realized—she did not want to stop. She was a jockey—at last! All that careful study of her father's riders meant she knew just what to do. As Jeto ran wild, she mimicked their position. She pushed her chest up from his withers and squared her shoulders, tucked up her legs, and shoved her heels down. As he sped down the furlongs, she shifted her seat to the center of his back and in a steady voice said, "Jetolara, it's me, Cheryl."

The fear in the horse's chest parted like clouds at the sound of his girl's voice. The visions of a bobcat or any other type of danger melted away, and he steadied his canter. Then he bounced to an easy trot. Then Jetolara stopped, turned back to look at his rider, and plainly begged her for some oats.

Huffing and sweating, her father arrived at the paddock's edge, her mother swift behind him, their faces stricken with worry. Cheryl dismounted. Jetolara followed her to them without so much as a lead rope, like a puppy, as she explained what had happened.

Then she startled her mother and father, perhaps herself most of all, with what she said next. "Papa, I love myself. And I'm going to be a jockey." She reached up to scratch Jetolara's long white stripe. "In fact, I already am."

Chapter Four

THE PACKAGE

Dinner at the White house was not the farmhouse affair you might imagine in prettily written story-books about countryside living, with a red gingham tablecloth spread with country cooking. It wasn't just that Doris Jean didn't have a jot of time or a lick of interest in performing the role of farmer's wife (and she didn't, as working an overnight shift in the Ball jar factory to pay for the horses and the farm and Drew's guitar lessons certainly took up enough of her time and brainpower). It was that she *adored* technology.

Family harmony was maintained by the fact that the couple decided early on that Raymond would have total say over the racehorses, and Doris Jean would have total say over everything else. So whatever was the latest, coolest, most high-tech gadget, she read all about it, had to have it, and filled her family's lives with it. And in the '60s, that gizmo was something that today is so common as to be totally unremarkable: the microwave.

When Cheryl was a teenager, few people had microwaves, which were a rather recent invention. The sparkly appliance in the Whites' kitchen, made by Litton Industries, was highly unusual. When it first arrived, Mr. White's jockeys kept marching up the horseshoe-shaped driveway after they put the horses away to ask if they could heat things up just to watch it work: a potato, a cup of joe, "A shoe, Mrs. Gorske? Just this once?" ("No! And get those manure-covered boots out of my house!")

And so, every night after the machine's arrival, dinner was a microwaved spectacle, the family gathered not around the table but beside the gleaming Litton, zapping their meal to toasty perfection. All the while, Doris Jean relaxed in the comfort of yet another prized technological wonder: her electric massage chair.

"Remember how you used to have to wait for hours for those pierogies to cook?" Doris Jean said to Raymond that evening, after Jeto and Cheryl's dramatic display. He had just taken a steaming plate of pierogies, a specialty from his wife's ancestral homeland, Poland, out of the Litton. The heavenly scent of the soft little dumplings stuffed with potatoes and cheese filled his nose. His wife guided him by the elbow and gestured for him to sit in her marvelous massaging chair; he raised his eyebrows, skeptical. She'd bought the chair, and while the family would gather round as she read the racing column in Cleveland's *Plain Dealer* newspaper every week, it was a well-established rule that it was her throne—and hers alone.

She smiled. He sat. "And remember how exhausted and unfriendly I'd be after cooking all that time?" she said. He speared a pierogi, raising it toward his mouth, but she stopped him before he bit into it. She tucked a napkin into his shirt collar, leaned down beside the chair, and pressed the button that made its soothing massage start. She smiled as he sighed. "Dig in," she said. He ate.

She waited a moment as he chewed, swallowed, and melted a bit into the lounger. Then she drew herself tall to stand over him.

"Do you know why you're enjoying this meal? This magical chair? This time together?"

Raymond finished his bite and looked up. "Um, because of the clever inventors at the Litton microwave company? That nice deliveryman who carried this enormous—amazing—chair up the porch steps? The electric company whose huge bills we pay to run these gadgets you love so much?" He rattled off his guesses, a half-smile on his lips.

Doris Jean was not smiling. Her husband tried again, this time sheepishly: "Technology?"

"The answer, Raymond, is: THE FUTURE," she said. "I don't love *technology*. I love the future. I love that scientists saw electromagnetic waves and in them saw a way to speed up cooking—something humans have been doing the same way since *fire* was invented! I love that Thomas Edison whipped up a lightbulb, and clever humans after him found a way to use that current to make life better." Doris's brown eyes flashed, and strands of her golden-brown hair fell from her bun. "I love that you and I, a Black man and a white woman, were wed years before laws allowed people of different races to legally marry. We saw the future. Not the present. A better future than a hateful past."

Raymond reached over the plush arm of the chair, found the button, and turned it off. He looked up into his wife's shining brown eyes.

"That is why I fill this home with technology— because science imagines a better, brighter future," she said. "That's the world I want our daughter to live in, Raymond."

He put down his fork. His wife was right; he knew that. And he knew in his heart that part of him was stuck in the past, trotting the same furloughs as his ancestors and feeling afraid to forge a new path.

"The time has come for a female jockey, and you can no more stand in her way than you can progress," Doris Jean continued to her husband. "The future is Cheryl."

Cheryl's jockey training began the next day. But the minute she mounted up, it was clear that all her careful study at her father's side had meant that truly she had been training to ride since before she had learned to walk. She was a natural, everyone could see, and not a single one of the men who worked for her father made a peep about Cheryl, now coming on sixteen years old, training beside them. Like the herd of horses, who had accepted Jetolara so swiftly after he proved he could not only keep up with but outrun them, the jockeys recognized Cheryl's talent and respected it.

Cheryl's job was to breeze the young racehorses. That is, she performed practice runs with them, keeping them at a moderate pace so they could stretch and build muscle and endurance, while preserving their energy. Racehorses weigh about 1,200 pounds, but the main bone of their legs, the cannon bone, is not much bigger than a human's femur. Their hocks, which are equivalent to humans' ankles, are only slightly bigger than ours. They are delicate running machines, carrying huge amounts of weight on spindly limbs. Proper, gentle exercise, moderate workouts, diligent strength training, knowing what is too much or too far—all of this is essential to protect these fragile animals of whom humans ask so much.

Cheryl knew that elsewhere young horses were sometimes pushed too hard; on some farms, an injured animal's pain was masked with medication to make sure he or she wouldn't miss a race. Cheryl knew that when racehorses were no longer useful for racing, some owners were likely to sell them at rock-bottom prices to who-knew-what futures. At the Whites' farm, Cheryl spent each morning in the barn with her mother, examining every filly and colt to make sure not a hair was out of place. If they did find anything concerning, the horse in question rested.

Those horses who could not race got new jobs. The big gray mare, Savannah Lily, for example, had turned an ankle in a pasture and would never run again. She became what was known in racing as a "pony," though she was still horse sized! A pony's job is to babysit nervous juvenile thoroughbreds at the track; experienced and wise, she'd walk softly beside the jigging youngster as her rider led him or her by a lead rope, holding them back from galloping off. The technique is known as "ponying." At the White farm, the horses were family.

Although her father had come around, he still kept Cheryl from sitting on his prized racehorses who were gearing up for the track—horses with big futures, like Jetolara. He told her she still needed more time and experience. Every morning when she and the jockeys gathered in the dark barn before the corkboard where her father pinned the day's horse assignments, she found she was always on the slower horses whose racing days were long past, like Savannah Lily. And while Cheryl was pleased to be riding thoroughbreds at last, by the time her seventeenth birthday came around that year, she was feeling held back. It was as if Savannah was ponying *her*.

The situation did not escape her mother's notice, though as the year went on, she seemed to have less and less time to join her daughter on dawn patrols at the barn. Instead, she asked Cheryl and Drew to go in her place, teaching them how to feel down a horse's narrow legs for heat that could indicate inflammation; how to soak a tender hoof in Epsom salt and water to draw out an infection; how to smooth white mud, called poultice, over a hock joint to cool away any aches. Doris Jean had been taking extra shifts at the Ball jar factory whenever she could; she often worked long days and then called home to tell the family she would miss dinner and ask if they could leave a plate of whatever they were having in the fridge for her to microwave later.

Then one morning, as Cheryl was inspecting the stalls and Drew was rattling the ceiling boards chasing cardinals up in the hayloft (mindful now, as everyone was, of the exact location of that trapdoor!), her mother entered the barn.

"Aren't you supposed to be at work?" Cheryl asked, surprised. "What happened to that extra early shift?"

Doris Jean smiled and pulled a parcel wrapped in brown paper from behind her back. Drew peeped down through the trapdoor and began to scramble down the ladder, as Sheba, his pup, bounded at its base. "I don't need those extra shifts anymore, honey," she said. "I was only working all that overtime to earn enough to get you this."

Cheryl raised an eyebrow. What high-tech thingamajig had her mom invested in now? "Thanks?" she said, confused. It wasn't her birthday, after all.

Cheryl took the package from her mom, sat on a hay bale, and gently tore apart the brown paper. It was not a gadget but, rather, something both very old-fashioned and yet newfangled at the same time: a jockey's silk competition blouse. But the material was a most flamboyant shade of orange, bursting with yellow polka dots; Cheryl had never seen anyone wear such flamelike colors in a race. She unfolded it. It looked just like the racing silks her father's jockeys wore, but theirs were red, with his initials on the back. She turned the shirt over: big orange letters read "DJG." Doris Jean Gorske . . . they were her mother's initials.

It felt like a cruel joke to hold the beautiful racing silks in her hands when it felt clear her father was never going to let her ride in a race. All this time she had been training and working, and still she had never even been allowed to sit on one of his competition horses! All Cheryl wanted was to become a licensed jockey, and now—after Olympian Kathy Kusner had sued the Maryland Racing Commission in 1968 over the unfair rule blocking women from racing—it seemed possible. It was 1970, and women jockeys had started to ride! Cheryl admired those pioneers even as she also noticed that none of them were Black, like her. But if her own father wouldn't give her a shot, what other racehorse trainer would? She had begun to lose hope.

"Why would you get me jockey's silks, Mom?" Cheryl asked. Tears began to well in her eyes, and they shone even in the dark barn. She clutched the orange silk in her fists. "To be a jockey you need to have a racehorse under you."

Her mother laughed softly. "I didn't work all those extra hours this past year for just a shirt!" She opened the barn door behind her a crack, just as Drew reached the ladder's bottom rung. He skittered out into the yard with Sheba and almost ran smack into a man who was leading a sleek, earth-brown filly out of a trailer.

"Hold your horses, young man!" he said. Then he turned to Cheryl and her mother. "Where should I put your racehorse, Mrs. Gorske?" the man asked. "Which stall is for Ace Reward?"

"Present!" Drew squealed at the horse, as Doris Jean squeezed her daughter's elbow.

"No, honey," his mother corrected him, and she beamed at her daughter. "The future."

Chapter Five

ACE

All that summer, Jetolara watched, perplexed, as his Cheryl spent all of her time with a new horse, Ace Reward.

It wasn't Ace who bothered Jeto. Ace was a fine friend, and after the herd put the filly through the same paces with which they had tested Jeto—making her sleep beneath the bopping buckeyes for a few nights before they welcomed her gingerly into their community—she was one of the family. Horses don't feel jealousy; in fact, they don't feel *many* things that we humans feel. Equines are never unkind, for the sake of it. They're never insecure about their own worth. If a horse is sour or rude, look to what ails him or her. You will find that the cause is never just because that horse has a lousy disposition. A sore foot is more likely the reason a gelding is in a bad mood than simply because he woke up on the wrong side of the stall that morning; a bellyache of a brewing tummy ulcer is much more commonly the cause of an irritated mare than a "bad attitude."

Jeto liked Ace just fine. Sometimes the two horses stood nose to tail, chestnut against bay, each nibbling the itchy spots the other couldn't reach between their shoulder blades, whisking the flies from each other's noses with their tails.

And yet, there was this funny feeling that Jeto got when he had finished his morning oats and waited to be saddled, only to discover for yet another day that his rider was not his Cheryl. He felt a tightness in his chest when he watched her hands rest lightly on Ace's flank as she worked the dust from the bay's fine fur, moving the currycomb in circles. And a pang hit the chestnut somewhere deep in his core when Ace and Cheryl blasted by at a gallop on the track.

Jetolara loved Cheryl White.

Why do horses love us? Why do they perform for us? What makes them dance for us in dressage, fly over fences for us, blast around barrels, and run for the roses in a race? It is certainly not a matter of force. They are 1,200 pounds of muscle; a girl like Cheryl weighs a tenth of that. No amount of force she could use could ever truly push a half-ton of horse around. Whether on a pony or a Percheron, no rider is ever really telling a horse what to do. It is a request, and the horse—as best he or she can—replies: "Yes."

How does that magic come to be? The answer is what Savannah Lily knew by instinct. No one taught her how to manage her herd; how to protect her spindly little foals, big mama mares, and goofy geldings from coyotes and bobcats; or how to make them feel safe. She had not become the alpha because she bullied anyone. She was the alpha because she was confident, because she strode across a field completely sure of who she was, and because she knew why she was there: to lead the herd to safety.

A good horseback rider behaves like that gray mare; she or he does not *make* a horse *do* anything. Instead, the rider leads a horse—from astride the animal—with supreme confidence and conviction and honesty. Being the alpha, whether horse or human, is not about being a boss. It is about guiding. And horses, prey creatures who need each other for safety in the big wide world, feel comfy when they have guidance. In that way, horses and their riders become a herd. A herd of two.

And so that pang in Jeto's heart was not exactly jealousy when he watched Ace stretch her rich brown body across the beaten furlongs, coil into a knot of energy, and then burst off again, over and over until she was so far off, she seemed no bigger than a buckeye nut. ("No!" he would whinny as he watched Cheryl, astride Ace, drifting farther and farther away with her horse's every powerful stride.) It was a simpler, far more pure feeling. Jeto wanted to be with his herd: Cheryl.

Most jockeys are paid to ride horses for owners like Doris Jean Gorske. But with her daughter, she made another arrangement: Cheryl had to pay. And the currency was A-pluses.

Good grades were a condition of being the jockey who would compete Ace, the debut member of Doris Jean Gorske Racing Stables. As the owner of DJG Racing Stables, Doris Jean got to select who would train Ace Reward and who would be her jockey. (Of course, one of her first moves was to "hire" the famous Raymond White Sr. as her trainer, paying him a fortune in microwaved pierogies.)

"Cheryl, you have to 'Ace' senior year at Grand Valley," her mother had said that first spring morning in 1970 when her racehorse arrived. "I need an ace on an Ace!" The contract was simple and binding: if Cheryl's grades dipped as she threw herself into jockey training, her mother warned, she'd lose the ride.

Cheryl heeded her mother's words . . . and set her sights. Every June one of Ohio's biggest horse races of the year was held in the village of North Randall. The setting was a venerable old racetrack,

Thistledown, on which jockeys had been testing their mettle since 1925. Riding her first race at Thistledown was Cheryl's goal. But making it happen wouldn't be as simple as hopping on Ace Reward and trotting up to the starting gate.

All jockeys must first earn a license to ride, and it's a rigorous path to win that right. First, each rider must become an apprentice jockey and spend at least a year learning the ropes. Fortunately for Cheryl, she'd basically been apprenticing all her life beside her father, so she had that out of the way.

Then there is a written exam, through which potential jockeys show that they've learned all of thoroughbred racing's many rules and regulations; Cheryl had essentially grown up in the backstretches of racecourses, accompanying her father to meets and matches all over the country. Her earliest memory was of her baby eyes blinking at photographers' flashbulbs in a winner's circle somewhere, cradled in one of her father's arms as he hung onto the lead rope of a stallion with his free hand and smiled for a picture of his latest win. She had been all of two years old, but that memory stayed with Cheryl because of what happened next: as the stud tossed his head excitedly, Raymond realized he needed two hands to keep him still for the photographers. Quickly he handed his tiny daughter up to the jockey, who popped her on the front, or pommel, of his saddle, and the reporters gasped, and cameras snapped. In a very technical sense, you could say that was Cheryl's first time riding on a racetrack—and she hadn't even been old enough to walk!

Cheryl's knowledge, however, was also by the book. Sometimes race days felt as if they dragged a little, especially when she was younger. If she was bored, the only reading on hand was often dry texts like the Ohio State Racing Commission rulebook. In the long hours between heats, she'd practically committed the entire thing to memory.

The toughest part of earning a license would be proving to the race stewards that she had what it took. Stewards in racing are like referees in sports, but they do a lot more. They are almost like judges and juries all in one. They watch races like hawks to make sure no rules are being broken, and they are quick to blow the whistle when they are. The stewards' job is to make sure horses and humans stay safe in the mad dash to the finish line, and the best way to ensure that is to make sure that the jockeys know exactly what they're doing.

Cheryl had read all about stewards in Cleveland's *Plain Dealer*, where reporter Ryan Peregrin wrote about the ins and outs of the sport. He was known as "Railbird Ryan" (*railbird* is a term for race fans who hang out all day long beside the track, gripping the fencing or rail at the thrill of every passing race). Railbird Ryan was must-read reporting for the White family, who would fight over who got to read the details of every race in his columns. The writer covered who won and who lost, of course, but he also explored what rules had been broken and which steward had blown the whistle.

Over the course of her time as an apprentice, Cheryl would get saddle time by doing things like taking young horses on field trips of sorts: her father would load up the fillies and colts and take them to local racetracks, to get the flighty animals accustomed to the noise and unfamiliar surroundings. That way, the pomp and circumstance of race day wouldn't faze them at all.

Apprentices like Cheryl would ride those horses around the tracks when the race was not on, teaching them to be brave. All the while, Cheryl knew, the stewards positioned around each track would be observing, making sure the apprentices handled their horses with grace and skill and that the hopefuls knew their stuff. And in the grandstands, the spectators would be watching, too, sipping mint juleps, the cocktail traditionally served at racetracks across the country. But it was not their eyes that mattered; it was the stewards who would decide if—when!—she was ready to run her first race as a licensed jockey.

Cheryl had her sights on being ready by the big June race at Thistledown. Almost as soon as Ace Reward trotted into her life, that goal was all Cheryl could think about. It became a refrain—*Thistledown*—that drove her to excellence. Kathy Kusner had gotten women into the starting gate. Cheryl would take Black women like herself across the finish line. She was determined to *ace* everything.

Filling buckets before sunup, Cheryl practiced geometry. She would measure the radius and height of a water trough with a piece of baling twine, then multiply the length together to calculate the volume of liquid. *Thistledown*. When the farrier came, she held unruly horses for him with one hand and read from the newspaper she held in the other as he hammered on horseshoes. When he finished and straightened out the crick in his back, the blacksmith quizzed her on current events. *Thistledown*. When the veterinarian doled out spring vaccines, she tagged along while the doctor explained the molecular structure of each medicine he injected. When he put away his syringes, he made her repeat it all back from memory. *Thistledown*.

At the edge of the big paddock was a makeshift starting gate Raymond Sr. had hammered together so the two-year-olds just learning how to be racehorses could practice. He would ring a bell just like at a real race—it sounded to Cheryl just like the school bell at the end of class—so the nervous baby thoroughbreds could get comfortable with the noise. Raymond White Racing Stables was known for horses and riders who could speed out of the gate without the hint of a stumble or delay; it's known as breaking "cleanly" from the gate. For Raymond, training was all in the details, and saving those few milliseconds at the starting line could mean the difference between winning by a hair or losing by a horse-length at the finish line.

Cheryl was practicing something else at the starting gate. Raymond White Racing Stables jockeys came from all over the country and around the globe to ride for Cheryl's famous father. As everyone worked to line up the horses at the gate, the jockeys would shout their home state or homeland to Cheryl. Her game was to respond correctly with their capital city before the starting bell rang. BUZZ! When she'd get it right, she'd WHOOP just as she and Earlene did in the Hill living room the night they found out about Kathy Kusner and her fight for equality. BUZZ! One stride closer to *Thistledown*.

As senior year began to wind down and graduation loomed, both Ace and Cheryl were at the top of their respective classes. The teenager was scoring top marks, while the filly was beating all expectations set by Raymond Sr.'s stopwatch. So it was a bit of a shock when Cheryl pulled her mother's yellow Ford Maverick into the Grand Valley parking lot (a tiny bit late; there had been horses to feed—and Ace and Jeto to pet!) to find Earlene Hill waiting out front, her face twisted with anxiety.

"The principal is looking for you, Cheryl!" Earlene said. "What a day to be late! Hurry!"

Earlene snatched her friend's hand and fairly dragged her up the high school's front steps, down the hall, and into Principal Gregory Huss's office. Cheryl was utterly lost. What had she done to be called in? She was getting top scores in everything, even phys-ed. For that, she credited Drew. Often, as the sun inched downward, she honed her softball skills with Drew on his homemade diamond in the pasture. Using the very apples he'd once pegged at her, her kid brother was now throwing fastballs for her so she could practice her swing.

"Miss White, I hear you are fixing to become the first female Black jockey," Mr. Huss said. He sat at his desk, his hands clasped before him, his voice measured. Cheryl had not even sat down. Earlene, standing a little behind Cheryl in the doorway, clasped her own hands behind her back and stared down at her own feet. Cheryl nodded to Mr. Huss.

"Well, Miss White, that will have to wait," Mr. Huss said, as Cheryl felt the blood rise around her collar.

Wait? Wait when, in the history of thoroughbred racing, there had yet to be a female Black jockey licensed in a race? Wait? Women had already waited until 1968—the year that Kathy Kusner had taken the sport to court—to be allowed to ride in races. All women like her had *done* was wait! Cheryl was racing for one reason above all: that unjust waiting needed to END. She felt like shouting.

But before Cheryl could open her mouth, Earlene touched her shoulder. "I did something, Cheryl," her friend said. "Don't be upset; it's because I love you, and I know what an incredible competitor you can be—on a horse and off one." Cheryl turned to face her friend. Earlene twirled a lock of her own hair around her fingers. "Cheryl, I entered you in *It's Academic*," Earlene said.

Mr. Huss stood up from his desk and walked around it, his palm outstretched. "Your friend Miss Hill has a good eye for talent, it seems," Mr. Huss said, beaming. "When the television producers contacted us, Grand Valley sent in your transcripts, your teachers' glowing recommendations, and your national exam scores." Cheryl's mouth still hung open a little. "Miss White, I know you've put in the work this year. Well, because of that, you're not just one of the top-ranking students in Ohio; you're one of the top students in the country."

Earlene threw her arm over her stunned friend's shoulder and squeezed as Mr. Huss gripped Cheryl's hand in his own and pumped it in congratulations.

"Young lady, *It's Academic* does not want you on its Ohio show or on its national broadcast either." Cheryl tipped her head to the side and stared as he continued to pump her hand up and down. "They want you to represent your country at *It's Academic International*."

Earlene began to bounce up and down, and though she was still a little floored, so did Cheryl. And you know what? So did Mr. Huss.

"The racing will wait—" He saw her face and hastily added, "But only a tiny, *tiny* bit longer, my young jockey! The show tapes just after graduation next month!" Mr. Huss said, now fully jumping along with the girls. "This summer you are going across the world: to Senegal, in West Africa! The competition is on June 17!"

Cheryl's bounce stuttered, but only for a second, so that no one else clocked it. THISTLEDOWN WAS TWO DAYS BEFORE! In that moment, the faces of her friend and her principal reflected back to her a teenager that Cheryl sometimes had trouble seeing: a person in whom they were confident and a girl who, to them, was already a winner. Cheryl White. She didn't want them to see hesitation cross her mind.

Thistledown was June 15! And the quiz was June 17! How was she to train to compete in that momentous race *and* study for such an important event as *It's Academic International*? Both of those endeavors required your whole body and your whole mind, Cheryl told herself. There was no way to do it halfway if you wanted to win. And Cheryl wanted to win more than anything in the world; she wanted to win both competitions. It seemed impossible. There, jumping for joy inside Grand Valley High School, the finish line had never felt farther away.

Chapter Six

DREW

Cheryl burrowed into her books; her father needed all hands on deck to keep Raymond White and Doris Jean Gorske Racing Stables running. That meant Drew was no longer able to chase cardinals around the hayloft or gallivant off with Sheba and his buddies for a game of apple softball in the pasture. The horses had to be fed.

Drew was tall for his age—roughly jockey sized—and strong from his young life spent clambering up gnarled apple trees and barn ladders. That meant that even though he was a fourth grader, he had duties like everyone else on the farm. And so each morning, while Cheryl was stuck in the house, poring over geography and memorizing important military battles and the names of world leaders, Drew was the one clanging the feed bucket and sending the horses soaring.

Drew also got to ride.

The first time he saw his name pegged to the corkboard in the barn, written beside Ace Reward, Drew was hit with an instant tummy ache. The bay filly was *Cheryl's* racehorse; he felt he had no business being atop his sister's thoroughbred. As he led the young horse out to the mounting block to get on, he glanced nervously at the gray house on the hill. He couldn't take his eyes off the kitchen window as he stretched into the stirrups. What if his big sister was sitting at the counter beside the microwave, nose in her book, and suddenly looked up and *saw*?

Cheryl *was* watching. Behind the soft linen curtains of the kitchen window overlooking the barn, she felt a pang, too. She was grateful her brother could pick up the slack for her while she buckled down and studied, but she wished, as people so often fruitlessly wish, that she could be two people at once: Cheryl the quiz champion *and* Cheryl the champion rider. As she peered out over the lush green hill rolling up to the barn door, she saw that spring was creeping toward summer and that the days were ticking by to the biggest tests of her young life.

Cheryl was a horsewoman, through and through, and that knowledge helped her persevere in her studies. Cheryl knew that young horses must grow muscle slowly, methodically, and deliberately, so that they are ready to burst from the gate on race day like a meteor. "A winning thoroughbred is a product only of its hard work," her father was known to say. She bent her pencil over her notebooks and pretended the scritch of her scribbling was a hoofbeat. In her mind her flashcards were a human version of breezing on the pasture track. She *did* see out the kitchen window, and she did hurt a little at the sight of young Drew, not her, astride the gleaming horses she loved so deeply. But the feeling was fleeting. She turned back to her books.

A winning thoroughbred is a product only of its hard work. A girl, too.

Back at the barn, Drew waited a few minutes until Ace began to pace with impatience. When no furious teenage sister came squalling out of the house, Drew settled into the tack. Like Cheryl, Drew had been riding ranch ponies all his life; but unlike Cheryl, who had never breezed a racehorse until their mother intervened, Drew knew his father was permitting him to ride these magnificent creatures for one reason—because he was a boy. Instead of feeling the surge of power—the joyful gift that horses give us when we sit atop their backs—Drew felt *terrible*.

Sheba looked up at him from beside the mounting block, and he couldn't meet the pup's eyes.

"'Drool.' That's what Cheryl calls me," Drew said to the little orange ball of fluff that had begun to trot boldly beside his horse's heels. As he spoke, the boy's eyes began to prick. He blinked and sniffed hard.

Cheryl had waited seventeen years and had begged and fought her way onto a thoroughbred's back. Drew was just nine years old, and he knew his way around an equine the way any child who grew up in a family that lived and breathed racehorses would. But frankly, he'd rather be tossing apples to Sheba or taking guitar lessons than riding horses. Yet his father had so easily set a kid like him atop a star thoroughbred, because he was *one* thing his sister wasn't: male. It felt so wrong.

"That's what I feel like now, riding her horse, Sheba. Total, terrible *drool*."

Part of him wanted to refuse the ride, to hand the reins to his father, to tell him that he'd been awfully unfair to Cheryl, and that every stride Drew rode felt mean. But the pride he saw in his father's eyes when his son put a foot in the irons stopped him. When he folded into the jockey's crouch position (called a two-point because just two points of the body—the thighs—touch the horse, and everything else hovers in the air), he could see his father beaming in his mind's eye. Raymond was passionate about horses, about thoroughbred racing, about the thrill of the gallop and the roar of the racetrack. But it was plain on his face that, above all, he was passionate about his son riding.

If anyone would have asked Ace Reward—and they didn't, of course (and even if they had, she wouldn't have been able to answer other than to stare hard with her big wet eyes and flick her talkative ears to-and-fro in gestures full of meaning that we humans can't understand)—she would have had her own thoughts on the matter. Ace Reward knew that Drew was no jockey. Drew was light like a jockey, tall for his grade, but still a kid. Nevertheless, he could crouch and hover over her saddle with his feet in the irons just like a race rider did. Ace recalled Cheryl mounting her just days before. That morning, the filly felt Cheryl ride with her whole body, her whole head, and her whole soul. Her hands on Ace's reins were steady and constant as they took to the pasture track, but so light that when she steered her around the other thoroughbreds on the loop, the filly almost felt like it was her idea to go left or go right. When they pulled up after that morning's sprint, Cheryl stroked Ace's long neck and rubbed her withers. Ace curled her lip in satisfaction. Cheryl's gentleness made her feel as calm as the horse did within her own herd, even when it was just the two of them cutting down the pasture track alone, flying out of sight.

Cheryl's body was so steady on her back yet moved with each clench and stretch of the filly's galloping stride. So much so that for long stretches of that gallop, Ace forgot her rider was up there; sometimes the horse felt Cheryl was a part of her.

Ace knew that Cheryl's brother was gentle, her brother was kind, her brother was steady. But in his heart Drew was not a jockey, and all horses, including Ace Reward, know the heart of whoever rides them.

So without meaning to, really, Ace Reward started to do something unusual for a young racehorse full of power and promise. She started to slump. While

Cheryl studied inside or stayed late after school with Mr. Huss for marathon trivia practice sessions, Raymond would watch his son breeze the big bay filly, his stopwatch in his hand. But about a week after replacing his daughter with his son as jockey, when the filly galloped by, Raymond glanced down at the watch, confused.

He held the watch to his ear: was it still ticking? This couldn't be right. The horse was at the height of her glory, she was worked daily by Raymond White, master trainer, and she was . . . slowing down? Trotting beside the racetrack after her boy, Sheba the Shiba Inu could almost keep up! The first week that Ace's times started slipping, Raymond had Doris Jean buy him a newfangled digital stopwatch to replace his old silver one, sure that the problem was that the timer was off.

No, it was Ace.

It wasn't that the horse didn't have the energy to go as fast as she did with Cheryl on her back, it was just that she didn't have the will. Why sprint if at the end of the race, she thought, your best friend was no longer there to throw her arms around you? What was there to run for?

As good as Cheryl was at coming up with answers— for example, the exact metric conversion of the forty-pound sacks of grain in the barn, the name of India's first president, the history of every horse in Jetolara's pedigree family tree going back five generations—Drew was good at questions. Drew had been endlessly talkative ever since he was little. And to be a good talker, you have to be a good asker; how else do you collect stories to tell? Between breezing the horses, the young boy would pepper his father's jockeys with questions about their homelands, their life stories, their hopes and dreams—even their favorite foods, right down to the ingredients. Whenever the blacksmith came, he hung around the farrier for hours, asking him how the coal furnace in his truck turned the iron horseshoes lava hot, why the molten horseshoes could then be shaped by a hammer, and why the sizzling shoes pressed onto a horse's hoof did not hurt the animal a bit.

When the veterinarian saw Drew coming, honestly, he would sometimes hide behind a hay bale. Can you blame him? The doctor needed concentration to do his procedures. If young Drew was there, he would ask so many questions that the vet worried he would miss a stitch or poke a needle into the wrong spot!

And so, after a week of riding his sister's racehorse while she crammed for the quiz show, all the while feeling the animal steadily slip behind when she should have been surging, Drew decided to do what he did best: question.

The sun was not yet up, and the farm was blue with dawn's darkness, when Drew rose from bed in the farmhouse and headed to the barn. It was May 17, 1971, and Savannah Lily was pregnant with the next generation of Raymond White Racing Stables' race-horses. She was nearly due. The evening before, she had showed the restless signs that the baby was coming, lying down, standing up, droplets of milk falling from her teats, as her body got ready to feed a hungry new foal.

Raymond had spent the night in the barn with her, as he did with all his mares when they were ready to give birth. He had sat up through the dark, snacking on toast—he loved it so toasted it was nearly black—waiting and waiting for a new bundle of joy. Drew found him there in her stall, wrapped in the coverlet that usually hung on the massage chair at home. His mother had brought it down overnight when the temperature dropped. Savannah Lily was dozing calmly, and aside from the fact that she was so round that she looked as if she had swallowed an entire hay bale whole, it hardly seemed like she would have a baby soon.

"Good morning, son!" Raymond said cheerfully when Drew peeped his head over the Dutch stall door. Though Raymond had been up all night, baby season was always so exciting, so full of promise, that he didn't need a drop of tea to stay bright and alert even on long overnights waiting for a foal to drop. "Savannah here is teasing me," he said. "After all that commotion last night, seems she's decided to bake that little one in her oven a little bit longer!"

Drew smiled. "She should try a microwave, Dad! It's way faster."

They both laughed loudly, making Savannah Lily snort herself out of her doze. Raymond scooched over in the straw, making space for his son to sit beside him. An especially thick layer of straw covered the birthing stall so it would be a soft and fluffy landing for the foal.

Drew inhaled deeply, seeking courage. The air was full of horse smells, of wholesomeness and peace. The boy sat down with a soft rustle, and Raymond threw the coverlet over both their shoulders as Drew snuggled up against his father's side in the dark.

"Dad," he said. "I have to ask you something. But I think the question may bum you out."

"Impossible," Raymond said, throwing his arm around his son's shoulder and pulling him closer. "Questions are the best. Every single day, I question myself: Am I doing right by each horse? Am I getting their training, feeding, and horseshoes just right? Do they have the right rider on their back? And are my goals the right goals for this filly or that gelding? You don't get to be Raymond White Sr., son, if you stop asking questions."

That felt hard for the young boy to believe. His father strode through every barn and into every winner's circle with such assurance, his legs slightly bowed from a lifetime of wrapping them around racehorses, but his stride full of swagger. Surely *the* Raymond White never questioned his own method, the boy thought.

"Dad, no one ever *dares* question you! Not even Savannah Lily, with all her sass, questions you! No *way* you question yourself!"

Raymond chuckled at the response, and father and son turned their eyes to the gray mare in the stall with them. She suddenly looked a little less snoozy and a lot more uncomfortable with her big, round belly. She stomped a hoof in the straw and slashed her tail against her side.

"Almost go-time, Mama!" Raymond said to the mare. He turned to his son. "The minute you think you know it all, that's when you can be sure you do not, kiddo. I'm always learning, and the best way to learn is to question, just like your sister is doing on that fancy quiz show, and just like you're getting yourself all worked up to do in this here barn. Now, shoot! What gives?"

Drew took a breath. He pulled the cover close as if it were armor against the consequences of the tough question he was about to ask his famed father. Except the minute he opened his mouth to speak, another sound echoed through the barn.

"Whiiiiiiinny!" It was Savannah Lily. With a groan, she dropped to her knees. Father and son threw off the blanket and jumped up excitedly, rushing to the sweet mare's side. It was time to welcome a new foal into the world.

Chapter Seven

ARISTIDES

"Dad, why is it so important to you that I become a jockey?" It was an hour later, and Drew sat cross-legged in the straw, the damp head of an infant foal on his lap, one hand cupped around his velveteen chin. The baby was stretched across the boy the way a Labrador retriever lolls across a sofa, his mother busily scarfing oats to get her strength back. Raymond was sponging off Savannah Lily's back legs and giving her compliments on a job well done. It had been a tiring morning, but the birth had gone well: the little tyke had stood up within fifteen minutes, as healthy foals must do. He wobbled on knobby knees as father and son guided the new creature to his mother's milk. Belly full, all that work of being born, walking, and snacking for the first time had tuckered him out. The baby had sunk gratefully onto Drew's waiting lap.

Few things are more peaceful than the first soft breaths of a brand-new foal: in, out, in, out—like waves wiping the sand clean or the breeze soughing through a cornfield, making it dance. Whatever had scared Drew about asking that question had drifted away on the gentle breath of the foal, and the warmth of the perfectly trusting, hour-old creature on his lap was better than any blanket-armor. "Dad? I said, 'Why is it so important to you that I become a jockey?'" he asked again.

The barn was quiet. It felt like the horses were listening, too. Then Raymond spoke: "Oliver Lewis."

"Huh?" Drew said. He looked up from the fuzzy foal in his lap and at his father at the far corner of the horse stall, confused. He wasn't sure if his father had heard his question. "Is that what you want to name Savannah's baby?" Then, more quietly, "But, that wasn't what I asked, Dad . . ."

Raymond emptied the last of the oats into the new mama's feed bucket, and she set about crunching away happily. He put the pail down in the straw and crossed his arms before his broad chest.

"Oliver Lewis," Raymond repeated. "That's the name of the man who was the first-ever winner of the first-ever Kentucky Derby, son, way back in 1875. He's why I want you to be a jockey."

Drew peered at his father; the baby horse sighed and shifted in his sleep. "What's some guy who won the Derby"—he stopped and counted on his fingers for a moment (Cheryl was the math whiz in the family, after all)—"ninety-six years ago have to do with me?"

"Everything!" his father boomed into the silent barn, startling the other dozing animals, like Ace

and Jeto, up and down the aisle, and Drew most of all. (The foal slept on. Being born was exhausting work.)

"Oliver Lewis was not only the first person to cross that famous finish line; he was Black, just like you and me," Raymond said, more reasonably now. "And in fact, for thirteen of the next fifteen years of that Kentucky Derby race, the winners *all* looked like you and me: they were Black men."

Drew grew wide-eyed. Though he was only a fourth grader, he had been tagging along at the racetracks with his family practically since birth; and even as a nine-year-old, he had long ago realized that almost no one on the backstretch looked like his father or him. The boy, too, understood heavy topics like prejudice and discrimination, treating people differently because of how they looked, because they were personal: his mom and dad had often told the siblings of the hardship they had endured to marry because Doris Jean was white and Raymond was Black. His parents had taught him hard truths about the world they grew up in, including that until just seven years ago, in 1964, laws all around the country forced Black people and white people to be separate. Segregation.

It hurt whenever Cheryl told him that there had been laws that said Black people could not dip in the same swimming pools or sit at the same lunch counters as white people, all the way until 1964. That was the year Drew turned two! There had been places where his mom and dad wouldn't have been able to swim or eat together? By law? It ached just to think about. So did his father's recollections about trips to some of the tracks down south, where he, a Black man, was allowed to race his horses but not sit in the owners' box to watch them run.

"Those jockeys were excellent riders, excellent horsemen, like Soup Perkins and Ansel Williamson," Raymond continued.

"Soup?"

"What a name, right? Pretty sure his real name was James. He was a Black man who won the Derby a few years later, when he was just fifteen years old! And 'Old Ansel'—that's what they called him back in his day—that was the man who trained Oliver Lewis's winning ride, a horse called Aristides."

Ar-i-STY-deez.

Drew mouthed the syllables to keep the strange name in his head.

"Now that was a great horse. What's more, Drew, Old Ansel had been born into slavery; he got free as a grown man and went on to train those two stars."

For the first time in perhaps his whole life, Drew was temporarily speechless. When he could form a thought again, it was yet another question, naturally: "So, so, where'd they—we—all go, Dad?" Drew asked.

"Well, those same nasty laws that tried to keep your mama and me apart, they pushed these people—these pioneers, really—who once were the top guys in the sport, off the horses, so to speak. Racist people wouldn't hire Black jockeys. Some of those elite riders ended up mucking stalls, for crying out loud! As for trainers, some states had laws that said Black people couldn't so much as step foot on their racetracks—how can you make a living if you can't be with your horse at the starting gate?" his dad said, his voice tight. "By the time I was your age, if other Black people were at the track anymore, it was mostly to pick up manure."

Drew raised an eyebrow, and Raymond knew his inquisitive son well enough to know what he was about to ask: *So how come we're still here*? "Well, kiddo, your grandpa was one of the few Black horse trainers who managed to hold on to his career. He owned his own horses, he had his own land, and he wouldn't budge." He scratched Savannah Lily's flank, smiling at the memory of his own pops.

"I like to think his skill was so respected, his horses so fast, that it was impossible to deny him a place at the racetrack. Oh, they certainly tried. But Grandpa persevered through a mixture of grit and luck, son," he continued. "Exactly what a thoroughbred needs to win."

He continued: "I ride for Oliver Lewis. I ride for him."

At that moment, the foal woke up and teetered to rest upright. The baby smacked his lips, and Savannah Lily nickered to him, as plain as day saying, "Breakfast is over here, kid!" in horse. Drew scooched out of the creature's way as the foal began the goofy, wobbly dance of moving forward on his brand-new legs.

Drew watched the baby teeter to his mother and begin to nurse. The boy couldn't imagine any better life than the one he had with his family on the farm in Rome and at the racetracks all over the country, with the thoroughbreds they loved so much. It was painful to know that so many Black people like him had been forced out of the same sport in which they had once been its stars.

He understood now why his father wanted him to be a jockey so badly. It was for all those people like him who could not—for Oliver Lewis and the Oliver Lewises who never got a chance.

Drew picked up the coverlet from the straw and pulled some strands off it. He tucked it under his arm. The other hand, he slipped into his father's. Together they crept out from the stall, quietly leaving the new mother and baby alone to snuggle and bond.

In the back of Drew's mind, another thought was forming. It was so, so unfair that across history, deserving people had been prevented from racing just because of who they were. Nowadays, you could say the same thing about another group of people who wanted to be jockeys, Drew thought: girls like his sister.

"Dad, I have a name for that colt," Drew said as father and son walked back toward their farmhouse, a fine mist kicking around their paddock boots. The sun was cinnamon-colored still, just peeping over the edge of the far pasture. The cardinals trilled their first soft notes to the dawn. "Let's call him Aristides . . . like Oliver Lewis's horse."

He would bring up that thought about Cheryl later, Drew promised himself. But for now, he was happy to hold the warm, brown hand of his father, the racehorse trainer.

Chapter Eight

THE NEWSPAPERS

The first reporter showed up on a Monday afternoon. She looked a bit out of place on the farm in heels that sunk into the grass and a business suit, her notebook flopping out from her purse. As she picked her way across the paddocks, one by one, the jockeys exercising the young racehorses hauled up their horses at the sight. Mostly it was because they were amused that she might step those nice heels into a pile of horse dung, but it was partly because it was strange to see *anyone* in a business suit on a horse farm. Boots and breeches and a nice coating of horse sweat were the typical uniform.

Even Ace Reward and Jeto turned their big heads toward the figure mincing down the slope, but they were mostly hopeful she had treats in her big swinging pocketbook.

"How can I help you, ma'am?" Drew asked, from up on Ace's back, hoping he sounded as grown-up as his dad. Raymond was up in the house fixing a torn saddle blanket on one of Doris Jean's newest gadgets, an electronic sewing machine with a computer chip inside that could zip out the niftiest stitchwork.

"I'm here from the *Columbus Dispatch*, son; it's a newspaper," she said.

"I read the papers! We've got a subscription." He felt a little miffed that the woman seemed to indicate that he didn't know his local newspaper, even though he was all of nine years old, so his response came out a bit rude. "But I prefer the *Plain Dealer*; my whole family reads the 'Railbird Ryan' racing column every week!" he said, crossing his arms across his chest atop Ace.

The woman started to answer, or perhaps gently explain to the huffy fourth grader who she was and what she was doing there in fancy clothing at severe risk of getting a coating of horse poop, when a car horn blared from up on the hill. A man came flying out of it—also in a business suit! He practically flung himself down the slope to where the jockeys and the horses were now all completely stopped and confused by the scene. Two people in pressed wool, nice shoes, and starched shirts on the farm in one day? It was too unusual. The man was sprinting now, and—*oof*, everybody winced—he plopped a foot right in a big pile of manure but kept on running toward them, his pinstriped suit flapping, his bright red necktie fluttering behind him like a cardinal's tail.

"Oh, no, you don't, Lucy Jane Lang!" he called to the woman, who had just whipped her notebook out of her bag and begun scribbling on it. "This is a *Dayton Daily News* scoop, not a story for you to steal for the *Columbus Dispatch*! I got this tip about the first-ever girl Black jockey first—which I just *know* you overheard me mention at the track this morning. I shouldn'ta said a thing, but I had one julep too many and started runnin' my darn mouth," he said as he came to the edge of the dirt racetrack in the paddock, scraping the muck from his dress shoes off on a fence post. "I saw the look in your eye. I *knew* you were going to rush to the Whites' farm as soon as I turned my back to focus on that race I had to cover for the *Dayton*. And *here* you are. You tricky thing, you, Ms. Lang!"

The woman smacked her free palm with her notebook in her other hand. "I object to that, Maximilian Solomon! How rude! I got this tip about this gal who is on the edge of becoming the first-ever female Black jockey *myself*!" Lucy Lang said with a huff!

"You're all *totally* ridiculous!" a voice boomed from behind the barn. A man in a three-piece suit and a fedora hat atop his head emerged from under the stables' eaves. As if all one creature, the jockeys' and their mounts' heads swiveled in the direction of the voice. Horse farms are necessarily places of quiet concentration, so commotion like this, with three separate strangers in fancy clothing hollering at each other across the hayfields, was very out of place. There would be no exercising this morning, horses and riders all decided simultaneously in their heads: whatever was happening here on this odd morning was all too interesting to miss!

"This is my newspaper's scoop; the *Plain Dealer* got it first. They don't call me Railbird Ryan for nothin'!" the man said, pointing a thick thumb at the shiny buttons of his vest. Drew almost fell off of Ace right there. *The* Railbird Ryan—the premier horse-racing writer in all of Ohio—was at his family farm? "But I don't see a Black jockette riding here?"

Railbird Ryan scanned the herd of men atop leggy thoroughbreds, all staring bug-eyed at him. Eventually his gaze landed on Drew. Before Drew could ask the question on his mind ("What, sir, is a 'jockette'?"), Railbird Ryan spoke again, to him: "You're no girl!" he said. "If I came all the way out to Rome for no story, you can bet that the readers of the *Plain Dealer* will hear all about it," he said darkly.

"Oh, no, no, Mr. Railbird, sir!" Drew spluttered out. "There is a girl jockey—j-j-ockette?—she's in the house studying. You see, she's a quiz whiz, too."

The three reporters in the paddock exchanged curious glances at each other, not understanding.

"I'll get her straightaway!" Drew shouted. And with that, he jumped off Ace Reward and ran for the house. In his excitement, he left the young thoroughbred standing there, her reins flung over her head, saddle on, very confused. (It wasn't a wise thing to do, but it was somewhat understandable for a kid meeting a celebrity journalist for the first time ever and perhaps getting a little overwhelmed.)

Luckily, Ace Reward was a very good horse. Finding herself loose and at her leisure, the bay thoroughbred chose to do her favorite activity: go find some snacks. And so she walked in no hurry at all, past the journalists, up the drive, and into the barn. The reporters watched the episode in shock, as the other jockeys got their heads straight and jumped off their horses. They scrambled to follow Ace, take off her bridle and saddle, and make sure she didn't get tangled in her reins. She did not. They found the filly in the barn, where she was already in her stall, expectantly waiting for someone to deliver oats like a customer at a restaurant.

In his notebook, Railbird Ryan scribbled:

RAYMOND WHITE RACING HAS THE BEST-TRAINED HORSES IN THE WORLD

Up in the farmhouse, Drew could hardly catch his breath, much less stammer out more than, "R-R-Railbird! RAIL. BIRD!" to Cheryl doing her studies at the countertop. Beside her, their father was working on the saddle blanket at the sewing machine. Both of them stared at Drew.

Then the door behind him swung open, and not one, not two, but all three reporters tried to step through it into the kitchen at the same time. As the Whites watched, mouths agape, the three people became a tangle of well-dressed legs and arms in the doorjamb. They had run up the hill after Drew, each of them *determined* that the others would not get to the story first. Once the three reporters worked it out between them and managed to get through the door, behind them poured in all of Raymond White's jockeys. They had swiftly thrown their own thoroughbreds into stalls and poured them fresh water before sprinting up the hill. Quickly they filed into the kitchen, each mumbling that he needed to microwave something—quite urgently.

The kitchen was crammed with nearly twenty people when Raymond White stood up from the sewing machine and said in the voice that the stoic man usually reserved only for very naughty racehorses, "WHAT IS GOING ON?"

The three journalists each began to speak at once, and phrases like "the story of the century!" and "this is *my* scoop!" pinged off the linoleum in one giant garble. Cheryl thumped her textbook closed and stood up, staring at her still-panting little brother, who was now clinging to Railbird Ryan's shirtsleeve. (He had one of Cheryl's notepads in his hand and was about to ask for an autograph.)

"Drool!" she said, addressing her kid brother. "What did you tell them?"

The hubbub was interrupted by a voice from across the room. Doris Jean stood in the living room door-way. "It wasn't Drew. I tipped off the local press about your race at Thistledown, honey," she said.

At the far end of the kitchen, the jockeys still clustered. They were all small men, as their profession required. Under Doris Jean's gaze, they all seemed to shrink smaller, suddenly aware of their boots tracking crud all over the linoleum floor. As one, the nearly dozen men smooshed into the kitchen started to head toward the door.

"Wait!" Doris Jean called. "Never mind your dirty boots; you know I'll make you come and clean up those tracks later, ha-ha! You all can stay. You racehorse men are a part of this, whether you know it or not, and I want you to be here to hear what I have to say." Raymond looked at his wife but said no more, as was his quiet way. In the pause as she drew breath to speak, first Lucy Jane Lang, then Maximilian Solomon, and then Railbird Ryan pulled out their notebooks and flipped to a fresh page. They hovered pens over crisp notepaper, ready to take down her words.

"Seventeen years ago, your father and I made a tough decision at the hospital where you were born," she said, turning to Cheryl. "The world was a divided place—and it still is in many ways—but those hateful divisions between people like your mom and your dad were law the year you were born, 1954. We loved each other, and while it was legal for a Black man and white woman to marry in Ohio, there were plenty of places where it was still not—the country repealed the rest of those laws in the country just four years ago, in 1967." The journalists scribbled furiously, desperate to catch her every word; they were not sure how this saga related to horse racing, but they were fascinated nonetheless. "Of course, segregation was law then, and prejudice was everywhere. Sadly, it still is."

Her husband reached across the sewing machine before him and squeezed her hand.

"And so, at the hospital, when it was time for Cheryl to be born, I went in alone, without my husband, so no one would give our new baby any trouble. And on Cheryl's birth certificate, for extra caution, we decided to list her as 'white.' I was afraid what might happen if I told the truth: that someone would be angry about who I loved and take it out on our beautiful Black girl." Doris Jean's voice caught in her throat.

Hearing his mother's words, Drew stopped tugging on his idol's shirtsleeve and turned toward his mother. He almost asked one of his questions, but he was so fixed on listening that he forgot to.

"Mom, I know you and Dad did what you felt you had to do to keep our family safe," Cheryl said, embarrassed that this room full of people was hearing her mother sharing this very private story. *That was seventeen years ago,* Cheryl thought. *That is in the past. Things are different now, aren't they?* But even as the thought formed in her head, she knew that prejudice was out there still, ready to rear its ugly head and snarl at her dreams.

On the racetrack that spring, Cheryl had become what's known as a bug, or an apprentice jockey, trying to learn the trade and earn her license. To do so, bugs had to get a minimum number of rides under their belts—hours of saddle time watched by race stewards—to show that they had the expertise to finally ride in a race to earn their licenses. Cheryl's turns were sharp, her splits from the starting gate were cleaner than most fully fledged jockeys, and she was personally trained by the best professional in Ohio—her dad. But she could barely find owners willing to set her atop their horses. Bugs were cheap labor, and by all rights, the owners should have been fighting for a bug with her family's credentials and her skill. But she could barely find even an elderly horse, or nag, to throw a leg over. She knew it was not her riding; she knew it was the color of her skin.

"Mama," she said again, "you did what you had to do. There is no reason to dwell on the past." Cheryl reached out her own hand and placed it atop the knot of her mother's and father's hands.

"I called each of these reporters here to tell a story about the future, Cheryl. I want them to set the record straight: the world was not ready for my gorgeous, brilliant girl when she was born, but it better be ready for her now—because she is coming for it at a dead gallop," Doris Jean said, her voice swelling. The reporters in the kitchen scritch-scratched in their notebooks, heads bent over the pages, getting down their quotes. "Cheryl is going to make history because she's a jockey. Because she is a girl. And because she is Black."

Doris Jean smoothed her own wispy hair. Now she trained her eyes on the group of jockeys still clustered by the kitchen door, wordless and staring. Some had taken off their helmets and were holding them to their chests solemnly, moved by the woman's painful words. "You all, scoot! Just look at those boots on my linoleum!" she said, clearing her throat. "Out of the kitchen. Our Cheryl has newspaper interviews to do!"

Chapter Nine

THISTLEDOWN

The filly's chocolate ears pricked forward, her shaggy forelock plaited up so that not a wisp of hair would block her vision. Ace Reward stood with every fiber of her being taut. If you had run a hand over her coat at that moment, the young thoroughbred would have felt as if she were made of granite or steel, under which ran the hot jets of rocket fuel.

It was race day.

"Of course I'm excited about the chance to be the first Black girl to get a jockey's license," Cheryl said from atop the filly's back. The filly couldn't help but jig a little under her. They were walking (well, thanks to Ace, prancing, really) in what's called the post parade. That is when all the racehorse contenders are led, riders on their backs, past the crowd in the grandstands and to the starting post. Cheryl was in her mother's loud orange silks, DJG on her back, her hair pulled back in a puff that poked out from under a helmet covered in the same silk. Goggles to protect her eyes from hoof-flung dirt were propped on the brim. She was speaking to a reporter . . . well, that was, to *one* of the dozens of reporters who were hanging over the track's guardrails, pointing microphones at her.

Doris Jean had been busy, and news of Cheryl's history-making ride had bounced around from Railbird Ryan's statewide report in the *Plain Dealer* to newspapers all across the country. It had since been picked up by television stations, leading their reporters to make similar pilgrimages to the Ohio farm in the weeks leading up to Thistledown. This ride was important because it was what is called a "probationary ride." Those vigilant stewards would be watching Cheryl's every move today: how she handled her delicate filly at the starting gate, how she instructed the horse to move safely at blazing speed between the ten other horses in the race . . . everything. It was not important that Cheryl *won* this probationary ride; it was essential that she *rode well*.

Ace had been in several races in her young life with riders before Cheryl. But she had never, ever seen grandstands so packed, and she had never seen these crazy contraptions that were being pointed at her over the rails. (They were television cameras, but try explaining *that* to a horse!) She shied uneasily at the fuzzy sticks that the reporters kept pointing at Cheryl's mouth. "They're just microphones, my girl; don't be scared," Cheryl told her in a low voice, and Ace calmed a little, not because she understood, but because she understood her girl.

Back on the farm in Rome, Jetolara paced the fence line, and no prodding from Savannah Lily's creamy nose could get him to stop jittering and join the herd cropping grass. Cheryl was not there, and neither was his friend Ace, and the gelding was concerned. Every inch of his equine body wanted his herd with him at all times, and two key members were missing. If horses could imagine (and we can't say for certain if they do or do not!), he would have dreamed himself taking Ace's place at Cheryl's first race and carrying *his* girl to glory. Instead, he strutted up and down in the pasture the day of Thistledown, wearing a deep rut at the paddock's edge like the furrow in a worried brow.

By the end of the day, the big bay had walked so many nervous steps that he felt as if he'd run a race himself. But none brought him closer to Cheryl, miles away, enduring the biggest test of her young life, without him beneath her. When he finally stopped pacing, it was when he arrived at this calming thought: Ace was a good mare, and he knew in his heart that she wouldn't let anything happen to her rider. Perhaps, Jeto thought as he at last relented and joined Savannah Lily and the herd tearing up mouthfuls of sweet grass, Cheryl was not just his, but horses and human all belonged to each other.

Thistledown was abuzz with news about the first-ever race of the first-ever Black female jockey. Tickets were sold out to watch her ride. A line of people not lucky enough to nab a ticket had formed outside the track doors to see if they could squeeze in anyhow. Under the green-and-white eaves of the grandstands, people were crammed shoulder to shoulder, craning to catch a glimpse of the star rider they had read so much about for weeks. Reporters had covered her every exercise run, cooling-out walk, and breezing ride in the weeks leading up to the race. The newspapers had flown off the stands, and readers gobbled up all they could about this exceptional girl about to make history. Even her kid brother had done interviews!

The people in the grandstands were from all walks of life. They were Black, they were white, they were Latino, they were Asian. They were old, they were young, they were male, and they were female. Some were gay. Some were autistic. Several of the people who came used wheelchairs. One woman enjoying a julep in the sun was blind. She could not watch the race, but she could feel it and hear it, and like the others, she was here to bear witness. She and all of these different people, and many more with differences known only to themselves, had come because of Cheryl. In her boundary-breaking ride, they each saw themselves. *If Cheryl can make space in the world for a person like her, maybe I can, too,* they each thought. Out on the track, getting ready for the race, Cheryl thought she was just a jockey. She did not know that she was an inspiration.

In the post parade, her father walked beside the pair of horse and rider, also answering questions. "I didn't urge her to become a jockey, but I have confidence in her ability," he told a reporter from the *Miami Herald* newspaper, who said she had flown all the way from Florida for the race. Cheryl heard his words, and her spirit wobbled slightly. It was great that he believed in her, but it reminded her of the resistance that remained. Because she was a girl.

"Miss White! Miss White! Spare a moment for the Associated Press?" one of the reporters called out.

Cheryl gently signaled for Ace Reward to halt, and the bouncy filly settled in front of yet another microphone. "Do you think you can compete against the guys?" the reporter asked bluntly.

Cheryl thought a moment. She stroked her bay filly's neck. "Ace here does, so why can't I?"

The newsman swung his microphone closer, almost thwacking Ace on her muzzle. It was too much for the jittery horse. She shied away dramatically, prompting a gasp from the reporters—that made it worse. Ace was up on two hooves! With her arms made strong from pitching hay bales down from the hayloft, mending fences, and riding unruly thoroughbreds, Cheryl held the reins firmly but without sharpness. Ace's roiling mind came back to Earth when she felt her rider, her herd mate, in control.

In a few seconds, she was on all fours again, ears popped at the reporters. The drama behind her, the horse was ready for another interview. Cheryl laughed;

she wasn't unsettled at all. She didn't reprimand her filly for her dramatic turn. She knew that humans ask a lot of horses—to be brave, to be fast, to be calm—and that it's important to know when we are asking too much. Ace needed to get to the starting gate, away from all this hullabaloo. "Male jockeys may have strength," Cheryl said to the Associated Press reporter with a little smirk. "But some horses might ride better with the tender hands of a girl."

But as she left the gaggle of reporters, Cheryl felt herself grow smaller. Here she was, having proven that she could get this far, and still, just before her big moment, people were questioning whether a girl like her was good enough. Doubt crept into her mind and wriggled around under her helmet. The times on her father's stopwatch said she was as fast as any jockey, but there were still owners who wouldn't give her rides. Who was right? All spring and summer, she had been focused on studying, trying to squeeze in rides on Ace in between, but Drew had been doing most of the breezing for her. Cheryl did not feel underprepared physically—she was strong and sharp and canny and tough as she had ever been—but mentally she was rattled. Her father's words. The reporters' words. And now, as the starting gate came into view, her own words to herself: *Do I belong here?*

"Cheryl! Cheryl! Over here!" Cheryl shook her head and came out of her spiral. It was her best friend, Earlene! She was wearing her best dress and hanging over the rail just steps from the starting post.

"You're here!" Cheryl exclaimed. Ace snorted at the loud yelp.

"Of course I am, silly. I'd even follow you to Senegal for the quiz competition if the money I make mowing lawns could buy me a ticket!" Earlene said, laughing. Then she quickly grew serious. As only best friends can, she saw in her friend's eyes that her smile was not genuine—that Cheryl was troubled. "What's wrong? This is your big moment, but I can tell your head is somewhere else."

Cheryl looked around. The other ten horses had headed into the starting gate. The race was about to begin. The gaggle of reporters was a ways down the rail, circled up around—who else?—Drew. He was telling them proud stories of how his big sister could pitch apples like no other, how she rode Jetolara bareback better than even Oliver Lewis could, and more. The buttons on his dress shirt were fairly popping off with pride. "You can tell me, Cheryl," Earlene whispered, staring up into her friend's eyes. "No one will hear; those reporters are too busy interviewing your kid brother. Boy, does Drool love to talk!"

Cheryl stroked Ace. The orange racing silks shone in the sun, but the inner light in Cheryl had dimmed. She spoke in quiet tones that sent Ace's radar-dish ears flipping back to catch the whisper. "What if they're right, Earlene?"

"About what, Cheryl?"

"That I don't belong," she sighed. "I wish I had been born a boy."

Earlene drew herself up tall. Her posture straight and her back rigid, her starched party dress looked like armor, and she a warrior. And she was. She was there, she knew right then, to do battle for her best friend. The battle was not just against the outside naysayers, but also against the more dangerous foes: the ones we let inside ourselves, the voices that tell us no before we even dare to try.

"Cheryl White, I said it once, and I will say it again. You can only be you, because everyone else is taken! A boy may have had an easier time getting where you are right now. He wouldn't have had to fight his father to become a jockey or deal with nasty owners not offering him horses to ride. But this *boy*, whoever he is, would also have been missing one important thing: he wouldn't have been Cheryl White." Cheryl began to crack a smile. "Cheryl White is my best friend, not some *boy*. Cheryl White is why those reporters are here, not for some *boy*. And Cheryl White is why those grandstands look like they might fall over because there are so many people stuffed in 'em!" Now Cheryl laughed.

"Everyone here loves you, Cheryl; you need to start, too," Earlene said more quietly. "And once you love yourself—the world is yours."

Cheryl took a deep breath. Under her, Ace did, too. The sound of a bugle pierced through the air. It was race time! She turned her horse toward the post, ready to load up in the starting gate. "One last thing, Cheryl." Cheryl turned her orange-topped head back over her shoulder to her best friend. "This is your moment, but it's also my moment—and a moment for all girls who look like us and so many more." Earlene was bouncing on her heels now as the two friends always did when they were excited. "When you light out of that starting gate, I want you to 'WHOOP!'"

Before you learn how the race went, it is important to know something. You must know that Ace tried. She really, really tried. And while in the world of horse racing, there are only winners and losers, in the rest of the world, it is not that black and white. There are merely different ways to be a person and different ways to be a horse. All have value, and all of us cross our own "finish lines" in our own way. The black-and-white quarter-mile markers—the tall striped poles that line racetracks—are regularly spaced and identical. Tracks are measured in a unit called furlongs, and each unit is 660 feet long. But in a life, those markers of achievement are not the same for every person. And comparing oneself as if you are running neck and neck like thoroughbreds, noses outstretched, trying to beat everyone else by a nostril, is not just silly, but it's also incorrect: almost everywhere *but* a racetrack, in all of life, there is no one finish line. Everybody has their own, and no two are the same. You can't measure life by furlongs. You can't win in life. And you can't lose. You can only grow.

Ace enjoyed running. She liked the way her hooves felt when they hit the packed earth of Thistledown: the duh-duh-DAH, duh-duh-DAH, of her own galloping stride, three beats when she really got going, and a moment of pure, hoofless suspension in air. Horses' feet move too fast for the naked eye to see their technical dance. They are a blur of motion. Back in the 1870s, way before video cameras were invented, and when photographs themselves were a new technology that Doris Jean would have swooned for, a photographer with the funky name of Eadweard Muybridge was determined to discover the pattern of a horse's footfall. He set up a fantastical contraption of cameras strung with trip wires and sent a racing horse named Occident galloping through. Muybridge captured twelve photos, one after another—Snap! Snap! Snap! In those photos, humans could at last see the truth: at the peak of a gallop, a horse does not touch the ground.

You don't have to have a contraption rigged of cameras and wires or a photo spread to tell any rider that. That stomach-fluttering moment when an animal stretches out in her full power is all the proof that anyone who loves a horse needs: these creatures can fly. The bay filly filled her lungs with fresh Ohio air, laced with electricity bouncing from the grandstands, down to the racetrack, and back again. And BUZZ! The starting bell rang: Ace was flying.

Cheryl did not "WHOOP!" as Earlene had suggested she do. She wanted to. She wanted to take that same deep breath as her horse and let it out into the Ohio evening, to cry out in that one sound: *Here I am! I love myself, and I am here!* She looked to her right and to her left at the ten horses and ten men on their backs, and she felt self-conscious and out of place. She already stood out enough, she thought. And so she stayed silent as they launched out of the gate.

Raymond had taught his daughter well. The pair broke from the starting gate clean—that means there was not a hair of hesitation, a stumble, or a single thing that delayed their launch into the race of their lives. That smart start meant they were out in front! Now, people often say, "The crowd roared," as if a crowd is some sort of wild beast! Well, as Cheryl and Ace sped down the first furlong, the filly's long brown neck—now her shoulders! now her haunches!—pulling ahead of the ten other horses in the race, the crowd truly ROARED. They became lions and tigers in the grandstand, roaring their joy; they became eagles and hawks, screeching with delight; wolves and bears growling, "This is our day!" This was the moment they had come for. To watch the jockey who meant so much to them succeed!

"And they're off! It's Ace Reward and everybody's favorite, Cheryl White, out in front, Cheryl White keeping a strong lead!" the race announcer's voice crackled over the loudspeaker, his words coming as fast as the thoroughbreds ran, so that they sounded like a jumble and all the crowd heard was *AceRewardandeverybody'sfavoriteCherylWhiteoutinfront!*

"Show 'em, Cheryl! Show 'em!" Drew called from the bleachers. The filly and the teenager were running hard down the first of six furlongs. They kept their lead as the second furlong passed them by; they blasted down the third and ate up the fourth— then, the fifth.

Oh, that fifth furlong.

The track rounded the bend as the horses came hurtling down it, the race two-thirds of the way over, the sweat slicking their necks and froth flying from their mouths. The strong, young thoroughbreds were having the time of their lives, running like it felt good to do so, running like they were born to. And then, at the fifth furlong—oh, that fifth furlong—Ace Reward got confused.

Ace had spent the past months breezing with Drew, while Cheryl studied for the big quiz in Senegal. Ace was a born racehorse, and she was happiest at a full-out sprint, but Drew's heart was not in being a jockey. And so, every day, when the pair practiced, the young boy would grow bored. Whenever he reached the far bend in the beaten pasture track at home, the farthest point from where his father stood with his stopwatch on the rail and where he was almost out of sight, Drew would quite often slow down. At the two-thirds mark on their six-furlong track at home, he would sing some of his guitar chords to the filly or recite his favorite baseball players' stats to her, or even, if his dad had ducked back into the barn to, say, hammer back on a lost horseshoe, he'd pull Ace up.

Then horse and boy would skedaddle off, making their own track across the pasture, following the red glow of cardinal wings in the grass and trotting after them until they flushed the birds out in a flutter of scarlet. Ace had no idea that those adventures were not—strictly speaking—authorized by Raymond Sr. In fact, Drew had taken her off course and slowed her down at the two-thirds mark to dillydally so often, she thought it was her *job*.

Ace tried. And to poor, mixed-up Ace, that will to try her best for her rider meant that she did as she thought she was always supposed to do. And at Thistledown, that meant that as soon as she felt that fifth furlong under her hooves, she put on the brakes. Hard.

The announcer's mouth had been full of *Cheryl-WhiteCherylWhiteCherylWhite!*, but as the eleven horses rounded the bend and began the final sprint toward the finish line, he didn't mention her once. It was his job to call the race leaders' names over the loudspeaker, to tell the crowd who was winning. But the girl in the orange silks had fallen so far behind that she didn't have a chance. There was no need to mention her at all. Cheryl was riding her hardest, but Ace thought she was doing her *job* when she let the herd of competitors pass her by, until they were a sea of tails and flicked-up dust. The pair was a horse-length behind the rest, then two, then three, then four, then five, then . . . Cheryl stopped counting. By the time the first horse slipped its nose across the finish, Ace and Cheryl were dead last. By eleven lengths.

Curiously, the noise from the crowd did not ebb when horse and rider slowly made their way to the end of the race. In fact, it grew and grew, and when girl and filly finally halted, panting and glowing with energy, you might have thought they had won. The grandstands rattled with applause. The very dirt in the track vibrated with joy, as if the racetrack on which they had run was itself celebrating.

Cheryl hardly heard it. She breathed out a deep, disappointed sigh. Her own breath was so loud in her ears that she thought that sigh came from the crowd itself.

Hardly anyone even paid attention to the actual winner of the race. He stood alone in the pen called the winner's circle, which is the area at the end of every track where top competitors go to have their win picture taken and collect their trophy. In fact, the photographer assigned the win picture that day was nowhere to be seen; she was off photographing Cheryl! And the newspaper reporters and television crews were surrounding her once again, too. In the scrum of people around Cheryl were her mother and father, Drew, and even bouncy Sheba. She caught eyes with Earlene, as her best friend ducked under a television camera to come close.

Cheryl burned under her orange helmet silks. She could not hear the cheers of the crowd. She heard one thing ringing in her ears: she had lost; she had lost; she had lost. That was what the newspapers would write. That was what the people would re-member. She had earned her license by successfully completing the race today, yes, but she had come in dead last. Why were they crowding around her? Why bother? She wanted to slink away, run home, bury her face in Aristides's fuzzy baby fluff for com-fort and never come out.

"Are you so happy right now?" a reporter asked her, another camera on a long boom dangling in her face. Earlene was ducking right beneath it, her hand on Ace's side, smiling and gently stroking the filly, telling her she was a good girl.

Cheryl scoffed. She sighed again. "For *losing*?"

Earlene looked up sharply at her friend. The girl had been overjoyed for her friend, thrilled to bursting at her achievement: Cheryl was now the first-ever licensed Black female jockey in the entire country, officially! She had done what had never been done, all through her own grit and determination. But hearing Cheryl say those words hurt Earlene's heart.

The people in the grandstands understood that today was a victory. Cheryl's parents did. Even young Drew did. But Cheryl did not. She may not yet have known how to win, but it was clear there as the dust settled at Thistledown that Cheryl White also did not know something that every jockey, every person, must know how to do when life doesn't go our way— as it so often does not.

Cheryl did not know how to lose.

Chapter Ten

SENEGAL

That sigh. That disappointed sigh. The one that she was sure rushed over the grandstands and down to the track at Thistledown. Cheryl believed she had heard that giant sound—the sound of the whole crowd sighing as if they were all one body—all at once at the moment she came in last. To her, the sigh-that-never-was was the loudest sound in the world. In her head, it was the sound of thousands of people exhaling their hopes and dreams simultaneously. It was a sigh that became a breeze. She almost believed it had buffeted her, high on Ace Reward's back, and ruffled the hair at the nape of her neck. Remembering it now, those let-go breaths were a gale-force wind that almost blew her off the thoroughbred.

Cheryl could not be convinced that the tremendous sigh she had heard was all in her mind. That no one was disappointed. That the people in the stands were happy just to see her there, to watch her ride, and to witness her try something that so many Black girls like her had never had the chance to try. And *she* had done it! But Cheryl could not be convinced. In truth, the sigh had come from deep in her chest, nowhere else. But it lodged in her soul.

And so, a couple of days later, she sat on her first-ever transatlantic flight, headed a whopping 4,292 miles away from her home in Rome, Ohio, to the city of Dakar, Senegal, in West Africa. Seated beside her was her high school principal, Gregory Huss; he had volunteered to be an *It's Academic* proctor. He wouldn't dream of missing this trip of a lifetime for Grand Valley High School's most famous pupil. But it didn't hurt that he got a free vacation to one of his favorite places in the world, Senegal, out of it as well! (As a young man, he'd been a journalist and had been stationed in Dakar, reporting for the *Plain Dealer*. His heart had leapt at the opportunity to return.) But above her principal's excited chatter through the long hours of the flight, that imaginary sigh was still all that Cheryl heard.

In the rushing wind blustering across the 747's wings as it cut through the air to the city at the western-most edge of the Sahara Desert, she heard that dis-appointed sigh again and again. As the wheels of the airplane deployed, she heard it in the whir of the gears. And when the plane landed, and it was time to alight, she heard it in the shuffling of the star-shaped leaves of the trees that grew at the airport's edge. The trees were like no other she'd seen, with trunks as thick as the grain silo back home. She knew from her studies that they were called baobabs. Sigh, the baobab leaves seemed to wheeze. She sighed back. Sigh. Sigh. Sigh.

It was hard to enjoy this moment, this incredible opportunity of going to West Africa to compete for her country in *It's Academic International*, on the heels of her loss. On the heels, she thought. That was all she had seen in the second half of the Thistledown race: forty sets of heels. Horses' heels kicking up dust in her and Ace's faces, as she trailed behind them when she *should* have seen nothing but the finish line, with every other horse in her wake.

Even the idea of moping through one of the biggest adventures in her seventeen years made her feel bad—because she felt bad about moping! Cheryl knew she should be appreciative; she was here in Senegal, surrounded by new things that made her heart thump with the thrill of discovery. She brightened as she settled into the black-and-yellow taxicab beside her luggage and Principal Huss, who pointed out all the incredible sights rushing by the cab's windows. There was the magnificent white presidential palace, its roof topped in emerald green like the grandstands of Thistledown. And just across from it, at the edge of the Atlantic Ocean, young men stood up to their knees in the water, scrubbing clean sheep and rams in the surf with the same loving care with which she rinsed off her horses. But it seemed whenever her heart raced with excitement, she heard in her pumping blood another sigh. Sigh. Sigh.

Thankfully there wasn't much time to dwell. Cheryl and Principal Huss's schedule was packed. After refreshing themselves with a quick gulp of sweet bissap, an icy pink hibiscus tea (mmm! Cheryl vowed to stuff her suitcase full of the dried flowers it was made of to bring back for her dad to drink with his blackened toast), they headed straight from the airport to the first round of the quiz show. It was that evening! Cheryl was nervous; the other kids had been there for several days, but because of Thistledown she had to hit the ground running. The competition was to take place in a former school building on Gorée Island, a small island off the city of Dakar's coastline.

During the plane ride, Principal Huss had told her all about the island. He painted pictures with his words: a seaside paradise of townhomes in hues as bright and multicolored as the racing silks of a herd of jockeys. The island was full of twisty streets, like something from a fairy tale, lined with mansions overhung with lush, manicured flowering vines in vibrant pinks and greens.

"It is as painful a place as it is beautiful," he said to her, as the flight attendant swept by, offering them packets of peanuts.

"What do you mean?" Cheryl asked, completely missing the offer of snacks.

"That pretty volcanic island has a history of abominable cruelty," her principal said. "During the slave trade, people from Europe kidnapped people from West Africa. They sold them into slavery. Gorée was known as the final place those stolen people were gathered. In fact, that old schoolhouse where the *It's Academic* final is being held was once a place where they held enslaved people before shipping them off to America."

Cheryl's face was tight with hurt. She knew that her grandpa's father had been enslaved. He had been forced to labor on Kentucky horse farms until the United States abolished slavery in 1865. He would tell fireside stories to his grandson of *his* father, who had been stolen from his home in Africa. And Raymond, in turn, had passed those stories to his family.

As the taxi pulled up to the ferry dock, and she glimpsed Gorée Island across a small expanse of water, Cheryl's body clenched. Once, people like her, her own ancestors, even, had been imprisoned here, she knew. A CLUNK! cut through her thoughts. A slim wooden boat, every last inch of it painted with colorful designs, swirls, and images, nosed up to the dock. It was deftly navigated by a man with a long pole. The word *Jërëjëf* was scrolled along its side. The boat owner's name, Cheryl assumed.

"First time visiting Gorée?" the ferryman piloting the boat said to Cheryl. He was so cheerful, and his face was so sunny that it soothed the haunting thoughts some. "Ever been on a pirogue?"

Cheryl looked at him: "A what? A pierogi? A Polish dumpling? My mom taught me how to make them . . . you like them, too?" Cheryl asked, *very* confused.

He reached out a hand. She clasped it and stepped down into the craft, wobbling a little. "Not a pierogi . . . a *pirogue*! That's the name of this kind of boat you're sitting in!" the ferryman said with a laugh. "*My* boat! Though I am partial to a good pierogi . . . mmm!"

Cheryl blushed at her mistake; Principal Huss stepped down, settled in beside her, and began chatting with the ferryman. A lanyard hanging around the ferryman's neck held his tour guide license, and he told her principal he specialized in history. Principal Huss immediately began boasting as he had to the flight attendant, the taxi driver—anyone who would listen, really—about his star pupil who had been selected out of the top-performing high school students in the country to compete in this international quiz event. He rat-a-tatted out Cheryl's big week. "If you're a historian, you'll love that your passenger here just made history!" he said to the ferryman, "Cheryl just became the first-ever Black female jockey to earn a racing license." If pride had a weight, Principal Huss was so full of it he would have sunk the ship right into the Atlantic Ocean.

The ferryman whistled a low whistle and looked hard at Cheryl. He was impressed.

Cheryl was quiet. She was stewing about her dumb dumpling mistake, which felt as if it symbolized so, so much more. She tried again: "Ah! You must be . . . Jërëjëf," she said to the boatman, stumbling a little over the unfamiliar word and gesturing at the letters painted brightly on the side of the pirogue.

"Not quite!" the man said jovially. He slapped his knee with his free hand, while with the other he shoved a long oar deep into the sand, pushing the boat out to deeper water. Then he busied himself with the engine in the back, until it spluttered and started.

"I'm Inua Toure! *Jërëjëf* means 'thank you' in Wolof, one of the many, *many* languages we speak here in Senegal." Now Cheryl was really embarrassed.

Inua saw the sheepish look on his passenger's face. "Oh, don't you worry, child. You aren't supposed to know everything!"

"But I AM, sir!" Cheryl almost yelled into the little boat, startling Inua and Principal Huss. "I'm here for *It's Academic!*" Her voice cracked, loaded with loss. "I'm here to win!" All that pent-up sadness, shame, and disappointment that had sighed and sighed through Cheryl in the days since Thistledown came pouring out as the pirogue bounced across the water.

Inua and Cheryl's principal exchanged glances. They were two men from different parts of the world, whose lives had been very different journeys, but like all grown-ups, they had learned lessons that Cheryl had not yet learned. In their exchange of glances passed the knowledge that at that moment, the teenager needed comforting. She needed to know that she was okay and that she would be okay, no matter what lay before her on that island or in life. Inua did not know about her defeat at Thistledown, but he did not need to. A creature in need of comfort, whether a horse or a human or even a ram, is plain to see, and they all require the same thing: care.

"Cheryl, you are here to participate in *It's Academic*," said Principal Huss over the churn of the motor. "You are here because you are smart, have worked hard, and deserve it. For no other reason at all." Cheryl shook her head. She was trying to listen, but she couldn't truly hear. Jockeys like her were supposed to *win*.

Cheryl sighed. They were nearing the island, and it was staggeringly beautiful. At the water's edge palm trees bowed. Principal Huss had been right, the shore was ringed by townhouses and mansions as brightly colored as Inua's boat, all draped in the pink rosettes of climbing bougainvillea vines and hibiscus petals.

"Just getting here is impressive, and I'm not talking about the work by your *excellent* ferryman!" Inua said with a chuckle at his own joke. "You know what this island once was; right, child?" he asked her, growing serious now. She nodded gravely. "Here you are, a Black woman, here for one reason: because you are great. You are our ancestor's wildest dreams. You don't even *need* to do them proud; you already have."

Cheryl felt her eyes prickle at Inua's kind words.

"Plus, you're not here just to win; you are here to learn," Inua said as he cut the chug-chug of the engine and returned to his oar, deftly navigating the craft to snub its nose into the sandy shore. Cheryl hung her head a little as he reached out a hand once again, this time to help her off the ferry. "In fact, you already have!" He smiled as he deposited her on the damp sand and then turned to help Principal Hess haul their hand luggage and step off the bobbing boat.

"Now what do you say to me, child?" Inua asked expectantly after they had safely debarked. In an exaggerated pantomime, he pointed at the painted words along the side of his pirogue.

Cheryl cracked a big smile, the first real one since she had arrived. Inua Toure was full of light, and in him she saw what she should have seen in the grand-stands at Thistledown: a person who believed in her. "Jërëjëf!" she said as he bobbed away in the water. "It means, 'thank you!'"

"STILL WRONG!" Inua called back, now unable to stifle laughs.

Cheryl stomped a foot on the sand where she now stood, peeved. "But you *said* that Jërëjëf means 'thank you' in Wolof!"

Inua Toure smiled mischievously. "Okay, okay, child, you got me. It was a trick question. It *does* mean 'thank you,' but that's not why I painted it on my pirogue." Standing beside Cheryl, Mr. Huss began to look impatient. They had to get going to the quiz run-through, and the first rounds of competition started that afternoon! They were jet-lagged, ferry tossed, and very nearly late!

"To me, Jërëjëf means something else, as well," Inua Toure said, as he settled into the captain's bench at the boat's stern, where he would wait to take customers back to Dakar's shore. "It is the name of my horse."

Chapter Eleven

JËRËJËF

Cheryl made it through three rounds of *It's Academic International* before she was eliminated from the competition on a question about the name of Hawaii's first king. ("King Kamehameha." It was a name that she'd not forget for the rest of her life. Grrr!) The competition was tough, with kids from France, Australia, Italy, Korea, Nigeria, Russia, and more, all vying to get to the final round the next day.

Something had shifted for Cheryl on that swift boat trip to the island, and she felt it when she looked around at that gorgeous, tragic island. She felt both its history and her own. And she felt proud to be there. Proud to be numbered among such smart kids. Whether she won or not, she could feel the pride that she should have felt at the finish line with Ace Reward—pride in her hard work and in herself, which did not rely on any outcome.

In the quiet chamber full of concentrating quizzers, she no longer heard that deflated sigh. *She almost heard a roar.*

It had been a grueling day of thousands of miles of flight and of little sleep. Cheryl and Principal Huss were bone-tired when they left the competition center. Wearily, they sat down at a table on the patio of one of the brightly colored houses on Gorée that had been turned into a seaside restaurant. Evening was touching on the bougainvillea and turning the narrow roads of the island gold. Teacher and student were tucking into steaming plates of thieboudienne, fragrant rice with just-caught fish that the chef had told them was the national dish of Senegal, when a colorful wooden skiff slid sleekly past the waterside terrace where they were eating.

"A celebratory dinner!" its captain called to them from the water. It was Inua Toure!

"Oh, hello, Inua! But not quite—" Principal Huss said through a mouthful of rice. "Our Cheryl gave them a run for their money but was eliminated just before the final round." He elbowed Cheryl playfully, as she quietly spooned rice into her mouth.

"Just what I was hoping! You have time for an adventure!" Inua said. He threw a line from the prow and looped it around the banister of the restaurant terrace. He called to the maître d', "Wrap up that thieboudienne to go, s'il vous plaît?" and beckoned to the two Americans to climb into his moored boat. "America's first Black female jockey has an African horse to meet!" Cheryl and her principal looked at each other. They climbed into Inua's boat.

Jërëjëf was not built like Cheryl's racehorses. He was plump and round where her thoroughbreds were sleek and wiry. He was short; his withers came up just to Cheryl's shoulders (and remember, Cheryl was jockey sized) where thoroughbreds were towering. His mane was cropped close, so it stood up along his neck, like the push broom in the barn; she could not imagine it ever submitting to her horses' race-day plaits. And he certainly lived differently. Her horses grew up in a green pasture. Here on the edge of the Sahara, where water was scarce most seasons, Jërëjëf's home was a dry lot not far from Dakar's ferry dock. The horse's view was breathtaking.

Inua had guided them up a hillside known as the Deux Mamelles, to where he stabled his horse. Looking out from the stallion's enclosure was a panorama of the endless Atlantic Ocean, the small dot of Gorée Island, and the sun sliding slowly into the sea. Inua had ducked into a dry-goods shop on the way to buy a sack of millet, fine grains that were rich in protein. Millet, Inua explained as he led them up the hill, took the place of oats and even hay here; in this dry climate, Jërëjëf needed a constant supply of nutritious millet to make up for the lack of green grass. The stallion spent much of his day with a nose bag of millet attached to his halter of soft braided cord, munching, munching. Cheryl thought Jetolara and Ace would have been in heaven: endless snacks!

Jërëjëf, or Jerry, as Inua called him, was a racehorse and a keen competitor, with wins at small friendly races between fellow horse owners that played out locally on sandy strips of beach. Lately, his proud owner said, he'd also received top honors in several official bouts at the racetrack, or hippodrome, as it was called, in Dakar's city center. Instead of carefully timed breezing each morning, Jërëjëf stayed fit by being a working horse. When he was not racing, he pulled a wagon for Inua. He was more reliable than any vehicle on the slopes of Deux Mamelles, with his careful feet placed just so on the rocky scree. "That's why I named him 'thank you,'" Inua said to her. "So every time I speak to him, I can express my gratitude for how much he does for me."

"That's a good name for *every* horse," Cheryl said.

The sun was dipping into the ocean when they arrived at Jërëjëf's hillside pen. The stallion was gray, his eyes outlined in a rich black that made them appear twice as deep and large. The tops of his legs had ever-so-faint zebra striping, an ancestral holdover from the wild horses way back in his family tree. There were no fence posts surrounding Jërëjëf. He was protected by natural boulders and the crags of the rocky hillside.

Principal Huss was a curious and intrepid man, having been a reporter. He was thrilled that he and his student had the opportunity to see a side of Dakar that was typically glimpsed only by locals, with Inua as their guide. But he was not a horse person and was generally skeptical of anything bigger than him. So when Inua suggested they help feed his horse dinner, her principal nervously turned down the offer. Instead, he took a seat on a rocky outcropping outside the pen and enjoyed the sunset over the Atlantic.

Cheryl was eager to pet Jerry's soft nose. She scrambled over a boulder, tugging the cloth sack of millet up with her. Atop the stone, she dipped into the bag. From her perch on the rock, she offered a fistful of the fine grains to the handsome little horse. Jerry wasted no time at all, scarfing every last kernel from her palm and then running his long whiskers between her fingers in case he missed a morsel. "Jerry, you're a greedy guy—just like Jeto!" she said, laughing as his muzzle tickled her hand. She sat cross-legged on the boulder and reached across the space between them gently. She combed her fingers through his forelock, which hung long and loose in comparison to his buzzed mane.

Jerry blinked at her. People spoke to the stallion in Wolof or in French, another language spoken in Senegal, but rarely in English. But to the small horse it all sounded the same. He did not know words, as no horse does, but he knew a horse person when he heard one. The calm timbre of her voice was accompanied by her steady, soothing touch. The millet was all finished, but the goodness was still there in her hands. The fine-boned stallion stepped forward toward the boulder Cheryl was sitting on, stretched out his muzzle, and leaned his tapered head into her lap. Jerry took a deep breath and sighed.

It was a sound of utter peace, and it erased the last of those other, phantom sighs, the sounds of self-doubt and self-loathing that had echoed in Cheryl's mind for her entire journey. The sun on the horizon was as red as a cardinal and flew low over the sea. The girl and the horse breathed together in the quiet.

Amid the peace of his in-out-in-out breath matching hers, Cheryl realized something: she never would have had this moment, with her new friend, the ferryman, with these stunning, dusty hills, with the red sun bouncing across the evening-dark Atlantic, or with Jerry—striped and squat and so beautiful—had she won *It's Academic*. Her third-round loss had not just given her a free day in this new country, but it also had opened up a path. It set her on a new journey. She didn't know it yet, but there on the hillside, Cheryl was beginning the important work of learning how to lose.

Jerry was a breed of horse called a Fleuve, Inua explained to Cheryl as they headed back down the hill, one of four native horse breeds in Senegal. They were hurrying a little to beat the setting sun. "It means 'river' in French," he said. "Because like a river, a horse is full of power you cannot contain." Senegal was full of that horsepower, he added, in between cautioning his new American friends to watch the rocky path as the shadows grew long before them—the country had more equines than anywhere else in West Africa. The other horse breeds, Inua said, were called the Foutanké, the M'Bayar, and there was a pony breed, called an M'Par. As they walked, Cheryl repeated the breed names in her head as if she were studying for a quiz.

"I wish the people on the backside of the racetracks back in Ohio or the owners of the racehorses who wouldn't let me ride could be here right now," she said aloud, but to herself really, as she walked. She kicked some pebbles in front of her. "I know that in the past, in Oliver Lewis's day, most jockeys and trainers were Black. But now there's hardly anyone there who looks like me, my daddy, or Drew at the racecourses back home," she said, navigating around a bushy Guiera shrub in her way. "Half the time, I feel like I don't belong there at all or that I'm not part of it. But here, it seems all the racehorse owners, riders, and trainers must look like we do at Raymond White Racing Stables."

"And I didn't even know West Africa *had* horses," Cheryl added. "Or riders."

Surprised with what he overheard, Inua wheeled in the track down the hillside. He had been leading his two guests, and they now stood blocked by him. His face was stunned at her words. "No riders, in West Africa? Child, where do you think, way back when, your American racetracks got their jockeys?"

She looked at Inua and then to Principal Huss as the sun slipped to the edge of the horizon. The light was purple now, and nightjars—the swallowlike birds that wake at dusk—flitted low on the hillside, looking for their breakfast. Neither of the men spoke, but they looked into her face intently; they were both educators, Principal Huss a teacher and Inua Toure a history guide, and they knew the best way to impart a lesson was to wait for the student to understand on her own.

"The enslaved people," Cheryl said slowly, working out her thoughts. "Some were riders, equestrians, and grooms, right? People who raised and rode the Fleuve horses, the Foutanké, the M'Bayar, and even little M'Par ponies!"

Inua nodded at her.

She continued, the words rushing out as she made the connections: "Ansel Williamson, 'Old Ansel,' who trained Oliver Lewis's Kentucky Derby winner Aristides—we have a foal named after him, Inua—he grew up enslaved." She looked out at the view over the ocean, at Gorée Island, the last stop for so many Black people before a terrible journey. That included, she just now understood, African horsemen who would later be sold to racehorse farms and tracks. Jockeys who had ridden in some of the first races in her homeland. Trainers who had taught magnificent thoroughbreds how to win. Grooms who had kept the animals healthy. All had been considered *property*, just like the thoroughbreds. She wished that she could hurl the boulders around her at the island and sink it into the sea.

Cheryl would remember Inua's next words for the rest of her life. She would remember them when she was riding thoroughbreds and other types of racehorses; she would hear his voice in every single one of the 3,160 thoroughbred races she rode in over a jockey career that would go on to last more than two decades. She would hear it in each of the 750 winners' circles she stood in, after each of the 750 races she won in her lifetime. It echoed as a reminder whenever she wavered with self-doubt. And his words resounded whenever she felt pride, like the day a grown-up Cheryl was inducted into the Appaloosa Horse Club's Hall of Fame for riding appys, a type of spotted ranch horse known for its blazing bursts of speed. Cheryl would remember what he said until the day she passed away in 2019.

"Horses are part of our history, child, and we are part of theirs," Inua said. He saw the comprehension in Cheryl's eyes as he gestured for the trio to continue on their way back down the slope; it was growing late. "They belong to people like us, just as much as anyone else. And you belong, too."

Cheryl looked deeply at her guide. Her words came out as a whisper. "Thank you," she said. "Jërëjëf."

At the base of the hill, the three parted with hugs; the sun had fled, and Cheryl's jet lag was fierce. Principal and student bid adieu to their new friend over a chorus of nightjars. As Cheryl and her principal sped to their hotel in another black-and-yellow taxi, near the peak of one of the Mamelles hilltops, a tough gray stallion lowered himself onto the soft sand of his enclosure. His belly full of his millet supper, he folded his tiger-striped limbs beneath him and closed his eyes.

Jerry dreamed of the young girl with gentle hands.

Chapter Twelve

THE SILKS

It was a long, hot Ohio summer on the White family farm. Cheryl was back to riding regularly, arriving to the barn at dawn to find her name on the pegboard next to, once again, Savannah Lily. The mare was slowly getting fit again after giving birth, and it was so fun to ride her because little Aristides always came along for the gentle exercise as she got in shape. He would trot beside his mother and her rider, loose, his stubby tail straight out with excitement, his nose drinking in the warm air.

Riding Savannah, long healed from her old injury, was a good way for Cheryl to get in shape for her next race: Waterford Park in New Cumberland, West Virginia. Riding Savannah was not as good as riding a racehorse at the peak of the game, to practice speed and learn from power, to perfect how Cheryl would leap from the gate and then this time *keep going* at the two-third mark of the practice track. But Raymond would not assign her those horses, and so she smiled and enjoyed riding slow Savannah with her sweet baby trotting beside them, while imagining they were galloping.

Ace had the summer off. It was clear that she had all the try in the world and that she was a good, dutiful horse, but after her performance at Thistledown and the glitch in her training, it seemed she had lost interest in going fast; she preferred exploring. That was okay, though; when one path doesn't work out for you—human or horse—it's important to be flexible and to try another. Life is winding and interesting and never goes where you expect it, and that's part of what makes it great. And Ace *was* great . . . just not great at being super-fast. It was decided that she would become a broodmare, like Savannah Lily, and have children of her own. As a mama, she would pass on her big heart, and all her try. Perhaps they could find a stallion to be the father who had the ambition she lacked. Cheryl could not wait to meet her racehorse's future babies.

Drew was also riding still, though he'd worked out a deal with his dad to do it in exchange for petty cash to pay for his guitar lessons. His heart was still not in riding, but with the incentive of a few dollars, he was much more focused. He didn't take breaks that could confuse young racehorses anymore.

Then one morning, Sheba woke Drew up uncommonly early, bouncing on his chest, ready to play. He slipped on his breeches and boots, and dog and boy bopped their way down to the barn. One lightbulb was on in the feed room, where Raymond was already awake and mixing up the grain for Drew to shake in his pail to call the horses in for breakfast as usual. Sheba scurried into the barn with Drew behind her, heading in to say good morning to his dad, when something caught his eye. The boy stopped short.

It was the corkboard. The riding list was already up, and his name was on it. And so was the name of the horse he was to ride.

Drew & Jetolara

Drew looked at the strong chestnut gelding in his stall. The horse's chocolate eyes stared back at him and blinked slowly. But in them, Drew did not see himself. He saw his sister.

He ran down the barn aisle straight to the feed room, with Sheba hot on his heels. The barn was dark, and the boy stood silhouetted in the doorway. His father was elbow deep in dry oats, stirring the feed. Drew did not say, "Good morning." He said two other words: "Oliver Lewis."

His dad looked up from his work, his eyebrows raised, his face puzzled. "Well, that's a new way to greet someone, kiddo," Raymond said to his son with a chuckle.

Drew was not smiling. He was holding his fists in two small balls, rooting his toes to the earth. He was standing the way a young colt does when it meets the herd for the first time, trying so hard to be very brave. He took a deep breath. Then he was very brave indeed. He told the great horseman Raymond White that he was wrong.

"Dad, you told me the story of Oliver Lewis, the first person to ever win the Kentucky Derby. You told me about all the prejudice Black riders like him and Grandpa and you faced and that we still face. Well, I'm standing here to tell you something, too." He took another big gulp of air and uncurled one fist to graze his fingers lightly on his puppy's orange head, to give him strength. "You, Dad, are being prejudiced against Cheryl."

Raymond stood up fully from his work at the grain bin. He dusted the oats off his hands and put his hands on his hips. He was of a mind to tell his son not to speak to him like that and to never throw such a hateful word around, particularly at his own father.

But he had raised Drew to ask questions, so that he might become a critical thinker, like Raymond himself. He was impressed by his son's verve, and he decided to practice what he preached. So he responded simply, "Please tell me what you mean."

Drew relaxed. Sheba banged her tail on the ground, sensing the tension slip from the air.

"Well, Dad, when one group of people are not allowed to do something just because of who they are, that's prejudice. That same history you told me about Black people like us in racing, well, that's kinda similar to how girls . . . women . . . have had it in racing, too. Isn't it? They weren't allowed to ride for so long for no reason other than who they were!"

Raymond nodded slowly. The one lightbulb in the tack room, dangling with cobwebs, was directly above his head. And as his face brightened with illumination from inside, it was almost as if its light was coming from within him, expanding like his mind and filling the room. He understood what his son was saying, and he nodded and nodded, trying to find the words. They didn't come. He was awash in pride over his young son's smart thinking—Drew's realization—and ashamed that he had not seen it himself at the same time. Shame and pride kept him nodding and nodding and thinking and thinking, surrounded by the soft smell of grain, the quiet sound of sleeping horses, and the deafening ring of the truth.

All this time, Raymond had known Cheryl was truly great. He had been tough on her in the same way as he was strong and disciplined with his racehorses: pushing them to their potential but never past it. He had kept her from riding his star horses so she would understand that her wins were earned not by the thoroughbreds she was riding, but by her. He had put her on the slow horses so she would learn how to make them fast, instead of coasting to glory on a proven winner. He had not thought that by making his daughter work harder for her dreams, his children would come to think he did not share them.

Drew spoke into the silence. "I will not ride Jeto-lara. I do not deserve to. He is the best racehorse we have, Dad. He should be ridden by the best jockey." Drew cleared his throat. "And the best jockey is Cheryl."

Raymond's eyes grew damp at Drew's speech and the love it showed for his sister. He nodded one final time, and then he spoke. "Drew, run up to the house and fetch your sister," he said. "You are absolutely right." As Drew scrambled out across the yard to get her, the sun inched up over the horizon. Its rays bathed boy, dog, and the resting horses at the bottom of the hill in warmth, the promise of another day. The blue-black of the August morning gave way to a honey-colored sky that grew to a deeper, brighter red as the day took hold. In moments, the whole morning was a brilliant, familiar red—the exact same hue of Raymond White Racing Stables' jockey silks.

Raymond knew just what he had to do to make this right.

Cheryl entered the barn a little groggy. It had been her turn to sleep late while Drew fed the horses their breakfast. But she brightened in an instant when she heard little Aristides whicker to her over the Dutch door of the stall he shared with his dam, or mother horse. She walked over to pet him, calling out for her dad, "Hey, Dad, you wanted to see me?"

Raymond stepped into the barn aisle, wearing his big barn coat. It was a little warm for the heavy jacket this summer morning, Cheryl thought, but perhaps her daddy had been up all night in the cool air tending a sick foal? She began to worry. "Everything alright? Aristides okay?"

"The horses are just fine, honey," he said. "But I'm not. I need to set the record straight, just like your mama did with those reporters before Thistle-down," He looked at her squarely, and she stopped stroking Aristides's tufted head. "I need you to know something: I have never doubted you," her father said.

Without meaning to, Cheryl snorted in total disbelief, as loudly as any startled horse. Suddenly, she was wide awake and so riled up that she couldn't help herself. She launched ugly words at her father. "That's a downright lie, Daddy! You stood in my path when I wanted to ride thoroughbreds. You gave Ace Reward, *my* racehorse, to Drool. At Thistledown you told the reporters that you 'never encouraged me.' And, and . . . and I know you always wished I was a boy!"

She began to cry. Tears were unusual for Cheryl, a person who never cried when the kids at school messed with her hair, when she came in last by those brutal eleven lengths at her first race, nor when she came home with a bronze trophy from *It's Academic*.

Cheryl admired her father and his quiet way with horses. She loved the way he listened and learned from others like her mother, the farrier, the veterinarian, the race stewards, and his team of jockeys; he was always sure that no matter how famed a trainer he was, he was never done learning. She could dismiss the rude owners and sour reporters who doubted she had what it took. But for such a man, for her own father, to challenge her goal of becoming a jockey . . . well, that challenged her very belief in herself. It had been a long hurt that built and built with every stride she rode. Now it came gushing out in a waterfall of fat tears.

"My child!" her father exclaimed. Little Aristides shot his head up at the sound and piped out a tiny squeak of a whinny. "Nothing could be farther from the truth! But now, it's so clear to me that I messed up. I went about this the wrong way if *that's* what you think."

In one step, he crossed the barn aisle, past where Aristides peeped his fuzzy snoot over the Dutch door, and clasped his daughter in his arms. He was a small man, jockey-built, and Cheryl was about his size, but he scooped her up in his strong arms. He lifted her like she was still his little girl, setting her down on a hay bale in front of the stall. He took a seat beside her, without ever removing his arms from that big embrace.

"I need to explain: your grandpa was a famous trainer, and it was only natural that I would follow in his footsteps. He popped me on his best horses even before I could walk, told anyone who would listen—the blacksmith, heck, the manure scooper, anyone!—that I would succeed him, like a prince takes the throne from a king." Aristides reached over the split door and took the tip of Cheryl's ponytail between his nubby baby teeth. She didn't notice. She was listening so intently. "And, yes, I did. But that left a hole in me. It left a smudge of doubt. Every ride, every win, I thought: 'Would I be so great, would I even be a horseman, if my father had not given me a head start out the gate?'"

Cheryl rested her head on his chest (after tugging her ponytail gently from where it was being gummed by the foal). "Of *course* you would, Daddy! You're the best there is!" She had stopped being mad, each tear taking some of the anger with it as they fell on the hay bale beneath her.

"Well, it took me a long time to come out of his shadow, to feel that way, to . . . you might say . . . love myself." In his arms, Cheryl squeezed him tighter. She so completely knew what he meant. "And I vowed to never do that to you, my dear daughter. I was stuck in my ways, I had my own prejudices to fight, you are right, but I always knew the truth: you have always been great, greater than me, maybe even greater than Oliver Lewis! And so, my dear girl, when I finally got right with myself, I decided I wanted you to feel that you earned every ride, not just because of who your daddy was but because of who *you* are."

Cheryl pulled away from him and sat up to look him in the face. She was surprised to see his face was also wet with tears. Father and daughter looked into the brown eyes they both shared, and new understanding passed between them. "When I told those reporters I never encouraged you, it was because I wanted them to know you make your own decisions and that you are your own woman—and jockey." He continued. "But I understand now that I went about it the wrong way; I hurt you. And I'm so, so sorry."

They sat quietly then, in the place that meant so much to father and daughter, the barn. They were surrounded by thoroughbreds, racehorses with careers behind them and in front of them, just as they were two jockeys, one who rode in the past and one who rode into the future. From inside his big barn coat, Raymond pulled out a brown paper parcel. It was flattened a bit from where Cheryl had laid her head on his chest.

Wordlessly, he put it on her lap. Aristides craned his stubby neck over the stall door, desperate to try to eat the wrapping. Cheryl gently tore into it. Inside was soft silk. Red and creamy white. Red polka dots going up the sleeves. She turned it over. There on the back of the jockey silks were three letters:

"Raymond White Racing Stables," her father said, "would like to formally hire Cheryl White to ride our racehorse Jetolara—in fact, we should have had her as our top rider all along. Will she accept?"

Cheryl nodded as the tears began to fall again.

"Good," her father said, holding back his own. "Because I was worried that she'd be our competition, and Cheryl White is unbeatable."

Chapter Thirteen

WATERFORD PARK

Does it matter if Cheryl White won the next race? Or for that matter, does it matter if she won a single race, ever? Does she need to have posed in the winner's circle, before the flashbulbs of eager reporters, smiling a nervous smile? Is it important if Jetolara bowed his big chestnut head for the garland of roses to be placed around his winning neck? What does it mean if she won? What does it mean if she lost? Would she be any less important? Would Cheryl be any less Cheryl?

"No!" said Cheryl as she sat astride Jeto in the starting gate at Waterford Park, answering the questions racing in her head. They had driven the horse truck in that morning across the Grand River to West Virginia. The deep green grass, or turf, of Waterford's mile-long racetrack wrapped around the packed dirt of the five-furlong racetrack she was about to run on. Cheryl's red silks flared in the sun, and the light glinted off the matching red-and-white-striped cloth on her helmet. She looked to her right and left at the jockeys settling into their starting slots beside her, concerned they had heard her say "No!" out loud. But they were intent, she saw, settling in their stirrups, soothing their excited mounts. She exhaled.

Jetolara was taut but steady beneath her. His deep eyes were focused through the bars of the starting gate at the dirt track ahead. If he was seeing the West Virginia foothills that climbed on the outskirts of the track—wisps of morning mist dragging at their peaks like stray strands of hay cling to a horse's lip—he gave no indication. He was a competitive race-horse, and every fiber of his thoroughbred soul was ready for action, no distractions.

But Cheryl's mind was flitting like those little red birds that so delighted her back home. It felt as restless as their crimson wings, touching here, now there, now everywhere, and back again. Her mind was in Senegal, with Jërëjëf in his sandy enclosure. It was back home in Rome, in the hayloft with rays of sunlight so bright and thick it looked as if you could strum them like the strings of Drew's guitar. It was with Earlene in the Hills' living room, cuddled on the shag carpet, watching their favorite programs. It was in Principal Huss's office, practicing quiz questions. It was in the massage chair beside her mother, reading the latest Railbird Ryan column. It was in the barn with her daddy, being handed bright red jockey silks.

She tried her old favorite pastime of doing math to cool her thoughts. How many feet in this five-furlong race? Well, eleven horses were in this race, with four feet on each of them, plus two feet on each jockey, so how many feet in this race? Well, if $11 \times 4 = 44$, and $11 \times 2 = 22$, then $44 + 22 =$ there are 66 feet! Right? Wrong! Trick question, Cheryl—

if a furlong is 660 feet long, then there are 3,300 feet in a five-furlong race! She laughed at herself for the little math joke she made up in her head. That calmed her a bit.

"Miss . . . um, miss?" said a tiny voice, no louder than a bright squeak. Cheryl looked around to where the voice was coming from. You heard a lot of things at the starting gate, some whinnies, some snorts, a few cusses, even, but you rarely heard what sounded like a little girl. Cheryl looked down and to the right, and there, far below her on the turf grass, stood a small child. She was no more than five years old, it seemed. What was a little girl doing here? The spectators were supposed to be far, far away in the grandstands on the other side of the track. Standing low and down near the horse hooves was dangerous for anyone, let alone an unsupervised child.

"You shouldn't be here! The race is about to start!" Cheryl exclaimed at her, shrill with concern. The little girl was dressed in tiny riding breeches complete with pink riding boots. A ball cap sat precariously atop her Afro. Someone had trimmed the brim and painted it pink and white to resemble a little jockey's helmet. "What's your name? Where's your family?"

"I'm . . . um . . . I'm Nikki, and . . . and they're in the grandstands. I snuck away. I'm . . . I'm sorry!" Nikki's lip began to tremble. In one hand, she had a tiny stuffed pink pony, and she hugged it to her chest.

Cheryl softened her tone. "Nikki, don't cry. I'm not mad, but it's not safe for you here. You'd better skedaddle back to your seat."

Nikki brightened a little, and her chin stopped wobbling.

"A child is at the starting gate!" It was the race steward, who had been loading another horse down the line into position. He came running across the width of the track, stumbling in the soft dirt in his haste. "You can't be here, little girl! What are you doing here?"

He reached the spot where Nikki was standing and, with a face full of concern, made a grab for her arm, but the little girl flung it out at him instead. He stopped abruptly. Clasped in her free hand was a piece of newspaper. It was the front page of the *Plain Dealer* from June 16, 1971, to be precise. Even from high atop Jetolara, Cheryl could tell it was the issue from the day after her race at Thistledown; she could see the words "First Black woman jockey . . ." on the page in Nikki's small brown hand.

Cheryl knew the lines of the article by heart.

"I want an autograph!" Nikki yelled with all her might. The race steward's face melted into laughter. "Well, aren't you somethin'?" he said to the little girl. He reached out and touched her baseball-cap helmet lovingly. "A race fan! You're a fan of this here jockette?" he asked.

"She's not a *jockette*!" Nikki retorted, sticking out her chin in defiance. Cheryl chuckled; she had hated that word when she saw it in newspapers and heard it on television programs about herself. She did all the same things her male peers did in the saddle; why should she be called anything different? The little girl stole her words, "Cheryl is a JOCKEY!"

The race steward put up his hands in mock surrender. "Okay, okay, little lady. Yer right. She's a jockey. But yer favorite jockey is a bit busy right now. How about we bring ya back to yer mama and papa, and she'll sign that newspaper for ya *after* she wins this here race."

He extended his hand to Nikki to lead her back to the grandstands and locate her family. As they began to walk away, Cheryl heard Nikki tell the steward that she planned to be just like Cheryl when she grew up, showing him her stuffed pink pony. "Do you know, sir, I can do *anything*?" Cheryl heard her say, as the steward nodded and anxiously scanned the bleachers for her family. When they were halfway across the oval of the track, Nikki stopped short. Her high-pitched voice cut back across the racetrack. "You promise I can have your autograph? After you win?" she called back to Cheryl.

"I promise!" Cheryl called in return. Nikki relented and let the steward lead her back to the bleachers, and Cheryl watched till she saw them reach the base of the steps. There, a worried-looking woman swept the little girl into her arms and then hugged the steward, too. Nikki had been found. Cheryl turned her concentration back to the race.

"I promise," Cheryl said again to herself. She had only a few seconds there at the starting line to think, but the feelings and thoughts crashed over her fast and strong, like waves hitting the ferry to Gorée Island. But Cheryl sliced through them, undaunted. As the man who was to ring the starting bell climbed onto a tiny platform at the race's start, the button for the bell in his hand, Cheryl knew the truth: she had promised the little girl she would win.

But she had already won.

BUZZ!

"WHOOP!" Cheryl called out as she and Jetolara shot out of the gate, clean and sharp, without so much as a hoof out of place—just as she had been taught and just as she knew in her jockey bones.

Cheryl had won. She had won when she shook that pail of grain that first morning and was greeted by Jeto's amber eyes and soft chestnut muzzle. She had won when she tumbled from the hayloft back home and landed on Jeto's broad back and rode the spooked horse safely across the pastures. She had won when she spoke up to her father about her true passion to ride. She had won when Jetolara gifted her his heart.

The first furlong fell behind them, and soon the black-and-white-striped quarter pole did, too, as Jetolara stretched his long neck out and flung out his hooves over the earth. He was every inch a thoroughbred on fire.

Cheryl had won when Earlene demanded she love herself. She had won when Principal Huss jumped for joy with her in his office at Grand Valley High School. She had won when her mother brought beautiful Ace Reward into her life. She had won when Drew had stood up to their father and insisted that Jeto was hers alone to ride.

That black-and-white blur beside her was another quarter pole, then another. The drumming of forty-four other hooves on the dirt filled her ears and pounded in her chest louder than her own heartbeat. "WHOOP!" she yelped to Jetolara, and he surged forward with the thrill, shouldering past racehorses on their left and right.

Cheryl had won when Inua Toure told her about the jockeys of West Africa and taught her the painful history of her ancestors, bringing her closer to truth. She had won when her father taught his children about Oliver Lewis, the famous Black Kentucky Derby winner and the legacy that he and they carried with them in the saddle. Cheryl had won when her father handed her his silks and shared his true heart with her.

They rounded the bend, and Jeto bounded forward, his rider hovering effortlessly above him, her back strong. Her legs—practiced from long rides on Savannah Lily and from chasing Savannah's unruly Aristides around the paddock when he wouldn't come in for supper—were like cords of steel. Her racehorse pulsed with exertion and drew in deep breaths of air. But breezing on the homemade track in Rome under her father's expert guidance had made him strong and tireless. He matched his rider's strength with his own.

Cheryl had even won when she lost on Ace Reward, she now realized, as the final furlongs at Waterford disappeared in their dust. That sigh she thought she heard in the grandstands that day—she now recognized it as a roar that her mind had twisted into something else. It was the roar only a winner gets, and she had won that day because of who had come to see the first Black female jockey ride. And she had won that day because all the people she inspired had won, too.

And so, as Jetolara blasted down the homestretch, as Cheryl pushed him on with her whoops and her laughter, she no longer cared if they crossed the finish line first. With all those wins behind her—she realized, laughing to herself at a gallop—she was the winningest jockey in history already. What significance was one more?

When Jetolara's nose crossed the wire, she barely noticed that they, in fact, *were* first. She was smiling, glowing, WHOOPING anyway, whatever the outcome. As Jeto strode into the winner's circle, there was Drew, with Sheba bounding around his feet; there was her mother in her bright orange race-day outfit; and there was her father, in crimson, fending off the reporters who wanted to know his secrets for training the first Black female jockey to ever win a race. But Cheryl didn't see any of that at first.

What she saw was a little girl. Nikki—gripped tightly by her mother now—was waiting for her autograph.

Cheryl White was the first Black girl in America to become a jockey. She won because she knew she would not be the last.

Author's Note

I'm Raymond White Jr., but you may know me better as Drew. I'm so proud to tell my big sister's story along with my coauthor, Sarah Maslin Nir. This book is based on the inspiring true story of how Cheryl became America's first Black female jockey in 1971—when she was just seventeen years old!

To tell Cheryl's story, we decided to add elements of fiction to help readers understand her pioneering journey from all angles—including through her race-horses' eyes!

Cheryl's story began on our family farm in Rome, Ohio, where our father, Raymond Sr., and mother, Doris Jean Gorske, ran a racehorse stable together. Dad's riders wore red and white racing silks. Our mother wanted to be able to easily find her horse during a race. True to form, her riders wore a novel color: bright, almost fluorescent orange and yellow silks.

Cheryl and I both began riding horses at a very young age, almost before we could walk. Riding horses was as natural as breathing, walking, or waking up in the morning. That story about falling on Jetolara from the hayloft and miraculously riding him to safety really did happen—but in real life, it wasn't Cheryl who tumbled onto him, it was me!

Our father did struggle with letting his daughter ride, but he came around because he knew talent when he saw it. "My girl is the best boy around this track," our dad said in the June 16, 1971, edition of the *Cleveland Plain Dealer*, after she lost at Thistledown on Ace Reward.

Cheryl was a math whiz, with an amazing gift and love for algebra. If being a jockey didn't work out, she wanted to become a math teacher. She did appear on *It's Academic*, a televised quiz show, but she did not go to Senegal to compete in an international version. That part of the book's journey, and the characters of Inua Toure and Jerry the stallion, were invented as a way to tell readers the story of enslaved Black equestrians who were purchased to become jockeys, trainers, and grooms. That history, and American thoroughbred racing's ugly past, is sadly all true.

Cheryl went on to win 750 races in her life. When her riding career ended, she became a racing official, working behind the scenes in numerous important positions. She studied hard, passing her steward's test with flying colors. Cheryl returned to the Thistledown racetrack, where it all began, as the clerk of scales and head of the jockeys' room in 2019. Later that year, she passed away unexpectedly, after suffering a heart attack. And now every year, at nearby Mahoning Valley Race Course in Youngstown, Ohio, a race is run in its most beloved jockey's honor, and our family presents the trophy.

All along her amazing career, Cheryl never forgot Jetolara, the horse who loved her best, and on whom she won her very first race. He and Ace Reward lived out the rest of their days on our farm in Ohio, as members of our family. —R.W.JR.

Acknowledgments

My first and foremost thanks are to my coauthor, Raymond White Jr., who picked up a reporter's call one day and ended up calling me family. I am forever grateful to the Whites for trusting me to shepherd this important story and for the honor of welcoming me into Cheryl's herd.

Thank you to Katherine C. Mooney, whose exquisite book *Race Horse Men: How Slavery and Freedom Were Made at the Racetrack* shaped my understanding of Cheryl's ancestral legacy; and to Dr. George E. Blair, founder of the Black World Championship Rodeo, and Mrs. Ann Blair, who both ran the New York City Riding Academy, where I worked in college. I am grateful to the Blairs for teaching me to properly pick stalls, but far more importantly, that Black cowboys were erased from American history.

Above all, thank you to Cheryl White, an extraordinary woman I so wish I had had the privilege to have met, for inspiring me and so many others. WHOOP! —S.M.N.

I want to give thanks to my father, my idol and role model from whom I learned the value of being humble.

To my mother, my biggest cheerleader, whose love for new technology I inherited.

To my son Raymond III, who taught me to be a father; I am so proud of the father and man he has become.

To my wonderful daughter-in-law, Nikki, the new matriarch and always "the voice of reason" in this family.

To my son Chris, the kind soul of the family who sees the best in everyone.

To my son Luciano, the baby of my boys, continuing to find his way in this world.

And, never to be forgotten, I want to thank my sister, Cheryl. We miss your laugh, your opinions (on everything, LOL), and just being able to call you. You are always with us and we will continue to have your legend inspire others. —R.W.JR.

SARAH MASLIN NIR is a reporter for the *New York Times*, a Pulitzer Prize finalist, and the author of *The Flying Horse*, the first book in the Once Upon a Horse series. She is also the author of the adult memoir, *Horse Crazy: The Story of a Woman and a World in Love with an Animal*. Second only to Sarah's love of horses, which she has been riding since the age of two, is her love of horse books. *The Jockey & Her Horse* is her second novel for young readers. She lives in New York City.

RAYMOND WHITE JR. hails from a family of racehorse professionals and has held almost every job there is in the racing world—jockeys' agent, exercise rider, assistant trainer, groom—except for jockey, like his sister, Cheryl—he was too tall! In addition to his equestrian roots, White is the father of Raymond III and daughter-in-law, Nikki, as well as Christopher and Luciano, and grandpa of Jocelyn, Raymond IV, and Sheena. He lives in Ohio with his two Shiba Inus, Sheba and Zoe, and Pablo the cat. *The Jockey & Her Horse* is his first book.

LAYLIE FRAZIER, a fine artist and illustrator who lives in Houston, Texas, created the cover and spot art for this book. Laylie doesn't ride horses, but she loves to illustrate them.

COMING SOON!

Book three in the
Once Upon a Horse series
will make its debut
in Fall 2024.

THE
STAR
HORSE

SARAH MASLIN NIR

art by LAYLIE FRAZIER

*A story about a horse who performs
onstage at the Metropolitan Opera,
and beyond, and the girl who loves him*

AVAILABLE NOW!

Book one in the
Once Upon a Horse series
has landed and is available
wherever books are sold.

"MOVE OVER, MISTY. SARAH MASLIN NIR'S
ONCE UPON A HORSE BOOKS HAIL A NEW
GENERATION OF EQUESTRIANS."

–PUBLISHERS WEEKLY

"CHARMING, BELIEVABLE (ESPECIALLY
WHEN IT COMES TO THE PRECISE MANNER
IN WHICH BOTH HORSES AND YOUNG
GIRLS THINK), AND JUST AS STRONG-
HEARTED AS TRENDSETTER HIMSELF,
THIS BOOK IS TRULY A CHARMER."

–PETER S. BEAGLE,
INTERNATIONAL BESTSELLING AUTHOR OF
THE LAST UNICORN

ONCE UPON A HORSE

THE FLYING HORSE

A girl & a horse
learn to soar

SARAH MASLIN NIR

art by LAYLIE FRAZIER